Classic Pages

Fable Garden
寓言花园

［美］艾玛·塞尔（Emma Serl）著
［美］哈利·E. 伍德（Harry E. Wood）绘
孟婧　张红梅　译

辽宁人民出版社

图书在版编目（CIP）数据

寓言花园：英汉对照 /（美）艾玛·塞尔
（Emma Serl）著；（美）哈利·E.伍德（Harry E. Wood）
绘；孟婧，张红梅译. —沈阳：辽宁人民出版社，
2024.7
（"世界儿童经典插图版"丛书）
ISBN 978-7-205-10836-6

Ⅰ.①寓… Ⅱ.①艾… ②哈… ③孟… ④张… Ⅲ.
①儿童故事—图画故事—美国—现代 Ⅳ.①I712.85

中国国家版本馆 CIP 数据核字（2023）第 168401 号

出版发行：辽宁人民出版社
地址：沈阳市和平区十一纬路 25 号　邮编：110003
电话：024-23284321（邮　购）　024-23284324（发行部）
传真：024-23284191（发行部）　024-23284304（办公室）
http://www.lnpph.com.cn

印　　刷：	辽宁新华印务有限公司
幅面尺寸：	180mm×210mm
印　　张：	9
字　　数：	160千字
出版时间：	2024 年 7 月第 1 版
印刷时间：	2024 年 7 月第 1 次印刷
责任编辑：	阎伟萍　孙　雯
装帧设计：	留白文化
责任校对：	冯　莹
书　　号：	ISBN 978-7-205-10836-6
定　　价：	79.00元

前言

这是一本由34篇小故事组成的寓言故事集。书中展现的是动物家园里引人入胜的小故事。每个故事短小精悍、隽永有趣又富有哲理,比如"百闻不如一见""欲加之罪,何患无辞""以其治人之道还治其人之身""鹬蚌相争,渔翁得利""三思而后行""己所不欲,勿施于人"等,可以让我们在学习语言的过程中吸取智慧,崇德向善,乐观进取。

这本书出版于1911年,由于年代久远,现传世极少,且全本几无。它在美国早已绝版,只有基于抢救性保护全球印刷作品的影印本存世,且缺字少页,售价昂贵。我们能够发现这个全本并在国内出版实属偶然且十分难得,堪为读者之幸。

这本书是为美国小学一、二年级学生编写的语言教材。

作者是一位长期从事小学英语教学的师范学校的学习方法教师。她能把世界上自古以来最广为流传的寓言故事用极为浅显的语言表述得如此娓娓动听，说明作者不仅具有丰富的教学实践经验，而且有深厚的语言学理论功底。所以，这本书当时在美国东部发达城市，包括纽约、波士顿和芝加哥等地同时出版并在很多小学里广泛使用。在当时，许多学校教师对这本书推崇备至。

我们将它呈现给读者，源于它有五个突出特点。

第一，正本清源。作为美国小学生母语学习用书和经典读物，这本书没有经过汉化加工，是美国本土学生使用的原汁原味、纯正地道的英语读物。学习和阅读它，让人如沐春风，有茅塞顿开的感觉，可以让我们知晓美国本土英语的本来面目。

第二，大道至简。本书仅用十分浅显的最常用的666个寻常英语单词就讲出了寓意深刻的不寻常故事，用最少量的简单词汇表达出完美确切的思想，为英语初学者在掌握几百个英语单词后就能与人进行有效沟通提供了实践机会。

第三，深入浅出。本书虽然用词浅显，却囊括了从实词到虚词、从时态到语态、从句式到句型的所有初级英语语法内容和语法现象。如果认真学习领会，可以让我们很轻松很轻易地全面掌握英语语法和语言表达方式。

第四，潜移默化。重复是记忆之母。在本书中，同一单词、同一句式、同一语法现象或反复出现，或间隔出现，或前后呼应，有过目不忘之感。这便于加深记忆，在潜移默化中记住了单词、句型和它们在特定语言环境下的具体用法。

第五，学以致用。因为是寓言故事，文中使用了大量的日常口语。所有故事多是以对话形式进行讲述，句子简单、简短、简易，阅读几遍后就能具备初级英语听、说、读、写能力。可以边学边用，可以速成，具有极强的实用性。

鉴于此，它是国内小学高年级、初中学生以及英语初学者难得的好读物。

任何著作都免不了瑕疵。原著中一些明显的瑕疵，译者在翻译过程中作了必要的更正；至于我们在翻译中的更多不足，恳请读者批评指正。

孟婧

2023年夏于大连

IN FABLELAND
WITH

LEO, the lion（列奥,狮子）
LOBO, the wolf（洛博,狼）
REYNARD, the fox（列那,狐狸）
BRUIN, the bear（布鲁因,熊）
BRUNO, the dog（布鲁诺,狗）
DOBBIN, the horse（多宾,马）
PUSSY, the cat（佩西,猫）
BUNNY, the hare and their friends.
（邦尼,野兔和它的朋友们）

ant（蚂蚁）bee（蜜蜂）bird（鸟）calf（小牛）crane（鹤）crow（乌鸦）deer（鹿）donkey（驴）duck（鸭子）eagle（鹰）fly（苍蝇）frog（青蛙）gnat（小昆虫）goat（山羊）grasshopper（蚱蜢）hawk（鹰隼）hen（母鸡）jocko（黑猩猩）kid（小山羊）lamb（羔羊）monkey（猴子）mouse（老鼠）ox（牛）rabbit（兔子）sheep（绵羊）spider（蜘蛛）tortoise（乌龟）

CONTENTS

1. The Lion and the Fox ...*012*
2. The Fox and the Crow ...*020*
3. The Wolf and the Kid ...*026*
4. The Dog in the Manger ...*032*
5. The Lion and the Gnat ...*036*
6. The Hare and Her Friends ...*042*
7. The Fox and the Grapes ...*048*
8. The Lion's Share ...*054*
9. Lobo and the Lamb ...*058*
10. Reynard and Mrs. Crane ...*062*

目录

一　狮子和狐狸　　　　　　　　…013

二　狐狸和乌鸦　　　　　　　　…021

三　狼和小山羊　　　　　　　　…027

四　牛槽里的狗　　　　　　　　…033

五　狮子和小昆虫　　　　　　　…037

六　野兔和她的朋友们　　　　　…043

七　狐狸和葡萄　　　　　　　　…049

八　最大的份额　　　　　　　　…055

九　狼和小羊　　　　　　　　　…059

十　狐狸和鹤　　　　　　　　　…063

11	The Dog and His Shadow	*...066*
12	How the Monkey Settled the Quarrel	*...070*
13	The Wolf and the Sheep	*...076*
14	The Cat and the Mice	*...080*
15	Reynard in the Well	*...084*
16	The Wolf and the Crane	*...092*
17	The Ant and the Grasshopper	*...098*
18	The Country Mouse and the City Mouse	*...102*
19	The Crow and the Pitcher	*...112*
20	Reynard and Pussy	*...118*
21	Lobo and Bruno	*...122*
22	The Quarrel	*...128*
23	The Blue Wolf	*...134*
24	The Lion and the Mouse	*...140*
25	Reynard and the Hen	*...148*
26	How Lobo Took Care of the Sheep	*...154*

十一	狗和他的影子	...067
十二	猴子是如何解决争吵的	...071
十三	狼和绵羊	...077
十四	猫和老鼠们	...081
十五	井里的狐狸	...085
十六	狼和鹤	...093
十七	蚂蚁和蚱蜢	...099
十八	乡下老鼠和城里老鼠	...103
十九	乌鸦和大水罐	...113
二十	狐狸和小猫	...119
二十一	狼和狗	...123
二十二	争吵	...129
二十三	蓝色的狼	...135
二十四	狮子和老鼠	...141
二十五	狐狸和母鸡	...149
二十六	狼是如何照顾羊群的	...155

27	The Hare and the Tortoise	...160
28	The Frog and the Mouse	...166
29	The Sick Lion	...170
30	The Wolf in Sheep's Clothing	...176
31	How Reynard Lost His Tail	...182
32	The Cat and the Chestnuts	...188
33	The Eagle and the Tortoise	...194
34	The Lion and the Echo	...198

二十七　野兔和乌龟	...161
二十八　青蛙和老鼠	...167
二十九　生病的狮子	...171
三十　披着羊皮的狼	...177
三十一　狐狸的尾巴是怎么掉的	...183
三十二　小猫和栗子	...189
三十三　老鹰和乌龟	...195
三十四　狮子和回声	...199
附录	...206

1
THE LION AND THE FOX

Leo, the lion, was King of the beasts.

Reynard, the fox, had never seen him. He thought he would ask the other animals about him.

He went to Bruin, the bear. Bruin was eating honey from a bee tree. He was glad to talk to the fox.

"Good morning, Bruin," said Reynard. "Have you ever seen Leo, the lion? I have heard that he is a dreadful animal."

"Yes," said Bruin, "I saw him once last summer. He is the most terrible animal you can think of. He is a hundred times as big as a fox. His eyes are like fire, and his teeth are like swords."

"I hope I shall never meet him," said Reynard; "I know I should

一

狮子和狐狸

狮子列奥是百兽之王。

狐狸列那从来没有见过他。他想,他会问问其他动物们有关他的事儿。

他去了熊布鲁因那儿。布鲁因正在吃树上蜂巢里的蜜,他很高兴和狐狸聊一聊。

"早上好哇,布鲁因!"列那说,"你曾见过狮子列奥吗?我听说他是个可怕的动物。"

"是呀,"布鲁因说,"去年夏天我见过他一次。在你所能想到的动物里面他是最可怕的。他比狐狸要大一百倍,他的眼睛像火球一样,他的牙齿像利剑一样。"

"我希望我永远不要遇到他,"列那说,"我想我会被吓

die of fright."

Then Reynard saw the goat. He was lying in the shade of a tree, chewing his cud.

"Billy," said Reynard, "did you ever see Leo, the lion?"

"Yes, I saw him once," said Billy. "His head is as big as a house. His mouth is like a cave, and his paws are like trees. Oh, he is a dreadful animal!"

"I hope I shall never meet him," said Reynard; "I know I should die of fright."

The next day he saw Pussy, the cat.

"Pussy," said Reynard, "did you ever see Leo, the lion?"

"Don't talk to me about him," said Puss. "It frightens me to think of him. I saw him once. He had just killed a deer. He is a terrible animal. When he roars the ground trembles. When he growls the trees shake. And when he walks in the woods the other animals run and hide."

"I hope that I shall never meet him," said Reynard; "I know I should die of fright."

"Listen," said Pussy. "I think I hear him coming. Yes, there he

死的。"

接着，列那见到了山羊比利。他正躺在树荫下，细嚼着反刍食物。

"比利，"列那说，"你曾见过狮子列奥吗？"

"是的，我见过他一次。"比利说，"他的头和房子一样大，他的嘴像山洞似的，他的爪子有如大树一般。哦，他是个可怕的动物！"

"我希望我永远不要遇到他，"列那说，"我想我会被吓死的。"

过了一天，他看到了小猫佩西。

"佩西，"列那说，"你曾见过狮子列奥吗？"

"可别和我提他了！"小猫说，"一想到他，我就害怕。我见过他一次，他刚刚杀死了一头鹿。他是一个可怕的动物，当他咆哮时，地面就会颤动；当他怒吼时，树木都会摇动；而当他在树林里走动时，其他的动物们就会跑掉躲起来。"

"我希望我永远不要遇到他，"列那说，"我想我会被吓死的。"

"你听！"小猫说，"我想，我听见是他过来了。是的，他在那里。跑呀，列那，快跑！"

is. Run, Reynard, run!"

But Reynard was too frightened to run. He lay down behind some bushes and nearly died of fright.

After the lion had passed on, Reynard came out of the bushes and ran home.

"He is more dreadful than Bruin or Billy or Pussy said he was. I hope I shall never meet him again," he said.

A few days later Reynard was hunting in the woods. Again he heard the roar of Leo. This time Reynard sat down behind a rock and watched him as he passed by.

"Well," said he, "that lion frightened me dreadfully, but he is not so terrible as the animals said."

The next morning Reynard was on the mountain. He saw Leo sitting in front of his den. He did not try to hide this time.

He walked up to the lion and said, "Good morning, Friend Leo. How are you this fine day?"

但列那已经吓得跑不动了。他伏在几簇灌木丛后面，快要吓死了。

等狮子走过去之后，列那从灌木丛中出来，跑回了家。

"他的样子比布鲁因、比利还有佩西他们说的可怕多了！我再也不希望见到他了。"他说。

几天后，列那正在树林里打猎，他又一次听到了列奥的

吼声。这一次,列那坐在一块石头后面,看着他走过去。

"嗯,"他说,"那头狮子可把我给吓坏了!不过,他也并不像那些动物说的那么可怕。"

第二天早上,列那在山上,他看到列奥正坐在他的洞穴前,这次他没有试图躲藏起来。

他向狮子跟前走了过去,说:"早上好啊,列奥朋友!今儿这天气真好啊!"

2
THE FOX AND THE CROW

One day Mrs. Crow found a fine piece of cheese.

"Here is a nice meal for my little ones," she said. "I will take it home to them. But first I'll rest in this tree."

Reynard, the fox, passed by the tree. He was on his way to the river for some ducks. He looked up into the tree and saw Mrs. Crow.

"Oh," said he to himself, "Mrs.

二
狐狸和乌鸦

有一天,乌鸦太太找到了一块美味的芝士。

"这真是我小孩子们的一顿美餐啊!"她说,"我会把它带回家给他们吃。不过我还是先要在这棵树上休息一会儿。"

狐狸列那从树旁经过,他正在去河边的路上,想去抓几只鸭子吃。他抬头向树上看,看见了乌鸦太太。

"哦,"他自言自语道,"乌鸦太太有一块精美的奶酪,我希望能得到它。也许我会得到它的,如果我能让她张开嘴,奶酪就是我的了。"

于是他大声说:"早上好呀,乌鸦太太,你今天看起来气色真好呀!我从来没见过你这么漂亮,你不愿意跟我唠几句吗?"

Crow has a fine piece of cheese. I wish I had it. Perhaps I can get it. If I can make her open her mouth that cheese is mine."

Then he said out loud, "Good morning, Mrs. Crow. How well you are looking today! I never saw you look so beautiful. Won't you talk to me a little?"

But Mrs. Crow did not say a word.

"I must try again," thought Reynard.

So he said, "Do you know what Lobo, the wolf, said about you? He said that you had a sweeter voice for singing than any bird in the woods."

Now this pleased Mrs. Crow very much. She was so silly as to believe all that the fox told her. She hoped he would talk some more, so she sat quite still and listened.

"Dear Mrs. Crow," said Reynard, "how I should love to hear your voice! Won't you please sing one little song for me? Then I will go to Leo, the lion, and tell him that I have found the Queen of Birds."

Silly Mrs. Crow know that she could not sing but she thought she would try. She opened her mouth and said "Caw, Caw," as loud

但乌鸦太太一句话也不说。

"我得再试试。"列那想。

于是他说:"你知道那头狼洛博说过你什么吗?他说你的歌声比树林里所有的鸟都甜美得多。"

当然,这让乌鸦太太非常开心。她太傻了,竟相信狐狸告诉她的这一切。她希望他能多说几句,所以她一动不动地坐着听。

"亲爱的乌鸦太太,"列那说,"我多么喜欢听一听你的声音啊!你不愿意为我唱几句歌吗?然后,我会去找狮子列奥,告诉他我已经找到了百鸟歌后。"

傻乎乎的乌鸦太太知道她自己不会唱歌,不过她想了想,她倒愿意试一试。她张开了嘴,尽可能大声地唱起来:"呱——呱——"

当她这样叫着的时候,奶酪掉到了地上,列那飞快地把它吃掉了。

"谢谢你,乌鸦太太,"他说,"给了我这么好的晚餐,那是我品尝过

as she could.

As she did so the cheese fell to the ground. Reynard quickly ate it up.

"Thank you, Mrs. Crow," he said, "for my good dinner. That was the best cheese I have ever tasted. Now let me give you this advice: do not believe all that foxes tell you."

的最好的奶酪了。好了,让我给你一个忠告吧:不要相信狐狸对你说的任何话。"

3
THE WOLF AND THE KID

A herd of goats were eating grass on the side of a hill.

"Don't go away," said a mother goat to her little one. "Stay here and the dogs will take care of you. If you go away, Lobo, the wolf, may catch you."

"All right, Mother," said the little kid; "I will not go far."

For a while he ate the grass near the others.

Then he said to himself, "what is the use of staying here all the time? This grass is dry. I can see some grass by the pond that is fresh and green. I am going down there. I don't believe Lobo is near."

So the little kid ran down the hill.

Now Lobo, the wolf, was hidden in the bushes near the pond.

三
狼和小山羊

一群山羊正在山坡上吃草。

"不要走开呀！"一只山羊妈妈对她的小家伙说，"待在这里，狗们会照看好你的；如果你走开，狼洛博没准儿会叼走你。"

"好的，妈妈，"小山羊说，"我不会远走的。"

有那么一阵儿，他一直在其他山羊附近吃草。

过了一会儿，他自言自语道："总待在这儿有啥意思？这儿的草都干枯了。我看到池塘边有些草，又鲜又绿，我要到那边去，我就不信洛博在附近。"

于是小山羊跑下了山坡。

这时，狼洛博就藏在池塘附近的灌木丛里，他正想逮点

He wanted to catch something to eat.

"There is a fine little kid," he said to himself. "I think he is coming this way. If he does I will catch him. What a fine dinner he will make!"

When the little kid came near, Lobo jumped out and caught him by the neck.

"Oh, Wolf," said the kid, "are you going to kill me?"

"Yes," said Lobo, "I am going to eat you for dinner."

"Before I die I should like to ask one thing," said the little kid.

"Well, what is it?" asked Lobo.

"I have heard, Lobo," said the kid, "that you can play beautifully on the horn."

"Yes, I can play a little," said Lobo.

"Then, dear Lobo," said the kid, "won't you play a tune and let me dance a little before I die? I love to dance."

儿什么东西吃呢。

"有一只活蹦乱跳的小山羊！"他自言自语道，"看样子正朝这边来呢。果真如此的话，我定能逮住他，那该会成为多么美味的一顿晚餐呀！"

小山羊一走近，洛博就跳出来并叼住了他的脖子。

"哎呀，狼，"小山羊说，"你会要了我的命吗？"

"是的，"洛博说，"我要把你当晚饭吃。"

"在我死之前，我想问一件事儿。"小山羊说。

"好吧，什么事儿？"洛博问道。

"我听说，洛博，"小山羊说，"你喇叭吹得不错。"

"是的，我是会那么一点儿。"洛博说。

"那么，亲爱的洛博，"小山羊说，"你能不能演奏一曲，让我在死去之前跳一会儿舞呢？我喜欢跳舞。"

"我从来没见过山羊跳舞，"洛博说，"不过我倒愿意为你伴奏一下。"

于是洛博吹起喇叭，同时小山羊跳起舞来。

"这很好啊，洛博！"小山羊说，"可是你能不能把声音吹得再大一点儿呢？我喜欢大声的音乐伴舞。"

于是洛博尽可能大声地吹奏。

"I never saw a kid dance," said Lobo, "but I will play for you."

So Lobo played and the kid danced.

"That is fine, Lobo!" said the kid. "But can't you play a little louder? I like loud music to dance by."

So Lobo played as loud as he could.

The dogs who were watching the goats heard the noise.

"What can be the matter?" said the leader. "Let us go and see."

They ran down the hill and there they saw Lobo playing and the poor little kid dancing.

The dogs at once jumped upon the wolf. Lobo dropped his horn and ran for the woods.

"How silly I was," he said to himself, "to play for that kid instead of eating him!"

正在照看山羊的狗们听到了声响。

"咋回事？"领头犬说，"让我们去看看。"

他们跑下山去，看到洛博在演奏，而可怜的小山羊正在跳舞。

狗们立刻向狼猛扑了过去。洛博丢下喇叭，向树林逃去。

"我是多么傻呀！"他自言自语道，"竟为了给那只小山羊演奏而没把它吃了！"

4
THE DOG IN THE MANGER

"I wish I could find a quiet place to take a nap," said Bruno one day. "The flies bother me in my kennel."

"Why don't you go into the barn?" asked Pussy. "It is cool there, and the hay is soft and sweet."

"That will be a good place," said Bruno. "I am glad you told me about it, Pussy."

In the barn he found a manger full of hay. He curled himself up there and was soon fast asleep.

At noon the oxen came home from their work. They were hungry and wanted the hay which was in the manger.

The dog woke up and snapped and growled at them.

四
牛槽里的狗

"我希望能找到一个安静的地方打个盹儿。"有一天布鲁诺说,"苍蝇老在我的狗窝里打扰我。"

"你为什么不到牛棚里去呢?"小猫佩西问道,"那里很凉爽,而且干草又软又甜。"

"那儿该是一个好地方。"布鲁诺说,"很高兴你告诉我这事儿,佩西。"

在牛棚里,他发现了一个装满干草的牛槽。他蜷缩在那里,很快就睡熟了。

中午,牛群下班回家。他们饿了,想要吃牛槽里的干草。

狗醒了,开始怒气冲冲对牛群吼叫。

"请走开,让我们吃饭!"一头牛说,"我们饿了。"

"Please go away and let us have our dinner," said one of the oxen. "We are hungry."

"I won't go away," growled Bruno. "I shall stay here as long as I like."

"You don't eat hay, do you?" asked another ox.

"Of course I don't eat hay," said Bruno. "Who ever heard of a dog eating hay?"

"Well then, get away and let us have it," said the ox.

But Bruno only barked louder and louder.

"You are a selfish fellow," said the ox. "You can't eat the hay yourself and yet you will not let anyone else have it."

"我不会走的!"布鲁诺吼道,"我喜欢在这儿待多久就待多久。"

"你不吃干草,是吗?"另一头牛问道。

"我当然不吃干草了。"布鲁诺说,"有谁听说过狗吃干草啊?"

"那好吧,你离开,让我们吃吧。"牛说。

但布鲁诺只顾一声高过一声地嚷叫。

"你真是一个自私的家伙呀!"牛说,"你自己不吃草,还不让别人吃。"

5
THE LION AND THE GNAT

One day Leo lay down to rest. A little gnat came and stung him on the nose.

"Go away," said Leo, "or I will hit you with my big paw."

"I am not afraid of you," said the gnat. "I shall stay here as long as I please."

"Do you say that you are not afraid of me?" Roared Leo. "You'd better go away. Don't you know that I am King of the beasts? I am stronger than any animal in the forest."

"You think you are too big and strong for me," said the little gnat. "I am small but I can fight you just the same."

"You fight me?" said Leo. "Why, I could kill a hundred gnats

五
狮子和小昆虫

一天，列奥躺下来休息，一只小昆虫飞过来叮在了他的鼻子上。

"滚开！"列奥说，"不然的话，我会用我的大爪子拍你。"

"我不怕你！"小昆虫说，"我愿意在这里待多久就待多久。"

"你是说，你不怕我？"列奥怒吼道，"你最好滚开，你不知道我是百兽之王吗？我比森林里的任何动物都更强壮。"

"对我来说，你自以为够大够强，"小昆虫说，"我是小了点儿，但我依然可以和你打斗一番。"

"你和我打架？"列奥说，"哎哟，我的爪子一巴掌就能打死上百只昆虫。"

"也许你可以做到，"小昆虫说，"不过让我们开打吧。"

with one blow of my paw."

"Perhaps you could," said the gnat, "but let us fight."

"All right," said Leo. "Go ahead."

Then the gnat stung Leo on his lip.

"There is my first blow," said the gnat.

Leo tried to strike the gnat with his paw. But the gnat was so quick that Leo hit his own face instead. His claws tore the flesh and made it bleed.

The gnat stung Leo in the corner of his eye.

"Did you feel that, King Leo?" he asked.

Again Leo struck at the gnat but only hit himself again. This time his sharp claw went into his eye.

"Never mind," said Leo, "I'll catch you yet!"

The gnat stung him on the nose.

Leo began to get angry. "I must hit quicker and harder," he said to himself, "if I want to catch that little gnat."

So Leo hit harder and harder. The gnat stung him again and again. Each time Leo hit himself.

At last Leo said, "I can't stand this any longer. My face is all

"好吧,"列奥说,"来吧!"

这时,小昆虫蜇到了列奥的嘴唇上。

"这是我的第一击!"小昆虫说。

列奥试图用爪子拍打小昆虫,但那只小昆虫的速度太快了,列奥反而打到了自己的脸上。他的爪子把肉撕裂了,流出了血。

小昆虫刺到了列奥的眼角。

"你感觉到了吗,列奥国王?"他问。

列奥再次向小昆虫打去,但只是又一次打到了自己。这次,他锋利的爪子刺进了他的眼睛。

"没关系,"列奥说,"我还是能捉住你的!"

小昆虫蜇上了他的鼻子。

列奥开始生气了。"我一定要出手更快速、更用力才行,"他自言自语道,"如果我想要抓住这只小昆虫的话。"

covered with blood and my eyes are nearly swelled shut."

He got up and ran away as fast as he could.

"Ho, ho!" Laughed the gnat. "Now, who is King, I wonder? Not the lion, I think."

Then the gnat flew away through the forest.

"I will stop here," he said. "This is a good place to rest a while."

He flew to a little bush and lighted on one of its leaves. But he did not see the web which Madam Spider had just finished spinning. His gauzy wings were caught in the silken threads.

"I am caught, oh, I am caught!" Cried the gnat.

He tried and tried to get free, but the web caught his wings and held him fast.

"I shall die and be eaten up," he said. "I cannot get away. I can fight a big lion but I cannot save myself from a little spider."

如此一来，列奥出手越来越狠，小昆虫一次又一次地蜇他，而每一次，列奥打中的却都是他自己。

最后，列奥说："我再也忍受不了了，我的脸上全是血，我的眼睛肿得快要睁不开了。"

他起身以最快的速度跑掉了。

"嗬，嗬！"小昆虫大笑，"现在，我想知道谁才是国王。我想，不是狮子！"

然后小昆虫飞过了森林。

"我要停在这儿，"他说，"这儿是个好地方，正好歇会儿脚。"

他飞到一小簇灌木丛前，停在了一片叶子上。但是，他没有看见蜘蛛夫人刚刚织完的网，他薄薄的翅膀被丝线缠住了。

"我被缠住了！哦，我被缠住了！"小昆虫叫道。

他试了又试，试图挣脱，但那张网缠住了他的双翅，紧紧裹住了他。

"我就要死了，要被吃掉了！"他说，"我逃不掉了。我能和一头大狮子搏斗，可我却不能从一只小蜘蛛手里救出自己。"

6
THE HARE AND HER FRIENDS

All the animals liked Bunny, the hare. She was so little and kind and good. She did not play tricks like Reynard and she did not tell stories like Lobo.

"I am your friend, Bunny," said Dobbin, the horse. "I would do anything for you."

"I am your friend too, Bunny," said the goat. "Call on me if you want anything."

"We are all your friends, Bunny," said the other animals. "We will help you at any time. You are so good."

"I am glad you all like me," said Bunny. "One cannot have too many friends."

六
野兔和她的朋友们

所有的动物都喜欢野兔邦尼,她是那么小巧、温和、善良。她不像列那那样爱捉弄人,也不像洛博那样爱撒谎。

"我是你的朋友,邦尼。"马多宾说,"我愿意为你做任何事情。"

"我也是你的朋友,邦尼。"山羊说,"如果有什么需要,就来找我。"

"我们都是你的朋友,邦尼。"其他动物们说,"我们愿意随时帮助你,你心地真是太好了。"

"你们都喜欢我,我真是太高兴了!"邦尼说,"朋友再多也不为过。"

一天,邦尼听说狗群要过来了。

One day Bunny heard the dogs coming.

"I must get away," she said. "If those dogs catch me they will kill me in a minute. I will ask some of my good friends to help me."

Just then the horse came down the road.

"Oh, Dobbin," called Bunny, "the dogs are coming. I am afraid they will catch me and eat me. You can run so fast; won't you carry me away on your back?"

"I should like to, Bunny," said Dobbin, "but I have to work today. Come to me some other time when you are in trouble. You have so many friends; ask someone else to help you. There is the donkey. Ask him."

"Oh, Donkey," cried Bunny, "the dogs are coming. They will catch me and eat me. Won't you carry me away on your back?"

"I am very sorry, little Bunny," said the donkey, "but I am not very well today. I don't feel like running fast. Someone else will help you. There is the goat. Ask him."

"Oh, Billy," cried Bunny, "the dogs are coming. Can't you hear them? They will catch me and eat me. Please carry me away on your back."

"我必须得离开！"她说，"如果那些狗抓住我，眨眼的工夫就会把我吃掉，我必须请我的一些好朋友来帮助我。"

就在这时，马沿路走了过来。

"哦，多宾，"邦尼招呼道，"狗要来了，我怕他们会把我抓住吃掉。你跑得这么快，你愿意把我背在背上带走吗？"

"我倒是乐意，邦尼，"多宾说，"不过我今天必须得工作，你改天遇到麻烦时再来找我吧。你有那么多朋友，请其他的朋友来帮助你吧。驴在那边儿呢，你问问他吧。"

"哦，驴子，"邦尼喊道，"狗要来了，他们可能会把我抓住吃掉，你愿意驮着我离开吗？"

"我很抱歉，小邦尼，"驴子说，"可是我今天身体不太好，我不想跑得太快，别人会帮助你的。山羊在那边儿呢，你求求他吧。"

"哦，比利，"邦尼喊道，"狗要来了，你没听见吗？他们可能会把我抓住吃掉，请你驮着我离开吧。"

"哦，邦尼，"比利说，"我倒是高兴这样做，但你看我的背太粗糙了，我担心会伤到你的小脚。绵羊在那边儿呢，他有着漂亮、柔软而又毛茸茸的后背，他可以背着你，你问问他吧。"

"Why, Bunny," said Billy, "I should be glad to, but you see my back is so rough. I am afraid it might hurt your little feet. There is the sheep. He has a nice soft woolly back. He can carry you. Ask him."

"Oh, Sheep," cried Bunny, "the dogs are coming. I am afraid they will catch me and eat me. Won't you carry me away on your soft back?"

"I cannot help you this time, Bunny," said the sheep. "You know some dogs bite sheep. I do not want them to see me with you. There is the calf. He can run. Ask him."

"Oh, Calf," cried Bunny, "the dogs are coming. I am afraid they will eat me. Please take me away."

"I should like to help you," said the calf, "but I am afraid to do so. So many older and wiser animals have refused you, I think I'd better not try. You know I am quite young."

"Well," said Bunny, "there is only one thing left for me to do. I must run. My own legs will save me if my friends will not."

"哦，绵羊，"邦尼喊道，"狗要来了，我怕他们会把我抓住吃掉，你能不能用你柔软的后背驮着我离开呢？"

"这次我帮不了你，邦尼。"绵羊说，"你知道有的狗是会咬羊的，所以我不想让他们看见我和你在一起。小牛在那边儿呢，他很能跑，你求求他吧。"

"哦，小牛，"邦尼喊道，"狗要来了，我怕他们可能会吃掉我，请带我离开吧。"

"我倒是愿意帮助你，"小牛说，"可我也害怕。那么多年长的和聪明的动物都拒绝了你，我想我最好也不要冒险了，你知道我还很年轻呢。"

"唉！"邦尼说，"我只剩下一件事可做了，我一定得跑。如果我的朋友们不愿意救我，我自己的腿能救我。"

7
THE FOX AND THE GRAPES

Reynard, the fox, was very thirsty. He had not found any water all day. He said to himself, "I shall die if I do not have a drink soon."

Sitting by the fence he saw Bunny, the hare.

"Oh, Bunny," he called, "come here. I won't hurt you. I want to talk to you. Do you know where I can get a drink? I am so thirsty."

"Yes," said Bunny, "I know where there is a nice spring of cold water, but it is a long way from here."

Reynard said, "take me to it, Bunny, and I will give you something."

"No," said Bunny, "I can't go with you. I am going after some cabbage. But you can find it if you go down the road to the big rock.

七
狐狸和葡萄

狐狸列那非常口渴,他一整天都没找到一点儿水。他自言自语道:"如果我不能尽快喝到一口水,我就要没命了。"

他坐在篱笆旁,看到了野兔邦尼。

"哦,邦尼呀,"他招呼道,"过来一下吧,我不会伤害你的。我想和你唠唠,你知道我在哪儿可以找到水喝吗?我好渴啊。"

"知道呀,"邦尼说,"我知道有个地方,那里有可口的冷水泉,但离这里很远。"

列那说:"带我去那儿吧,邦尼,我会给你报酬的。"

"不!"邦尼说,"我不能和你一起去,我要去摘卷心菜。不过,如果你沿着这条路一直走到大石头那儿,你就可以找

I am in a hurry, so goodbye."

Reynard hunted and hunted for the spring but could not find it.

Then he met Lobo, the wolf.

"Oh, Lobo," he said, "do you know where I can get a drink? I am so thirsty."

Lobo said, "no, I do not know where there is any water but I know where there are some nice grapes. I ate some once when I was thirsty. Jump over this fence and run up the hill. You will find them there. I am going to catch a sheep. Goodbye."

Reynard found the grapes but they were in a high tree.

"What fine juicy grapes!" He said. "How sweet they will taste! I shall not be thirsty after I get some of them. I cannot climb the tree but I think I can jump and reach them."

So he jumped and jumped.

"This is hard work," said Reynard. "I wish they were not so high."

Then he jumped again and again.

At last he said, "I cannot get them. But I do not care. I know they are sour grapes."

到它的。我要赶时间呢,再见吧。"

列那四处寻找那处泉水,但没有找到。

这时,他遇到了狼洛博。

"哦,洛博,"他说,"你知道我在哪儿能找到一口喝的吗?我太渴了。"

洛博说:"不,我不知道哪里有水,但我知道一个地方,那里有一些很好吃的葡萄。有一次我口渴的时候吃了一些。你跳过这个栅栏,跑上山去,就能在那里找到它们。我正要去抓羊哪,再见。"

列那找到了葡萄,但它们在一棵高高的树上。

"多么美味多汁的葡萄

啊！"他说，"吃起来该会有多么甜啊！我摘下来吃一些就不会渴了。我不会爬树，但我想，我可以跳起来够到它们。"

于是他反复地跳了又跳。

"这可太不容易了！"他说，"我真希望它们没长这么高。"

接着他一次又一次地跳起来。

最后，他说："我吃不到葡萄了，但我不在乎，我知道它们是酸葡萄。"

8

THE LION'S SHARE

Reynard stopped at Leo's home one afternoon.

"Oh, Leo," he called, "are you at home?"

"Yes, I am here," said the lion. "What do you want?"

"The donkey and I are going hunting," said Reynard. "We want you to go with us."

"I shall be glad to go," said Leo. "I was just wishing for something to eat."

So the lion, the donkey, and the fox started out together.

They had not gone far when they caught a fine large deer.

"Let us rest here and eat it," said Leo. "I am hungry. Donkey, you divide it. Give each one the part he should have."

八
最大的份额

一天下午,列那偶然从列奥家路过。

"哦,列奥,"他叫道,"你在家吗?"

"是的,我在家,"狮子说,"你要干什么?"

"我和驴子正要去打猎。"列那说,"我们希望你和我们一起去。"

"我当然愿意去了,"列奥说,"我正想要找点儿东西吃呢。"

就这样,狮子、驴和狐狸一起出发了。

他们没走多远,就逮到了一头体型巨大的健壮的鹿。

So the donkey took the deer and divided it into three equal parts.

"Now I think the parts are even," he said. "Which part do you want, Leo?"

Leo looked at the parts. Then he grew angry.

"What do you mean, Donkey, by taking so much for yourself?" He said.

"The parts are even," said the donkey. "If you don't like the way I have divided it you need not take any."

This made Leo still more angry. He sprang upon the donkey and killed him.

"Now, Reynard," he said, "there are only two of us. See if you can divide the deer."

Then Reynard put all the meat in one pile except a little piece of the leg. He put this off by itself.

"This big pile is your share, Leo," said Reynard. "This little piece of the leg is mine."

Leo was very much pleased with the fox.

"Reynard," he said, "who taught you how to divide the deer so well?"

"The dead donkey taught me how," said Reynard.

"让我们在这里休息一下,把它吃了吧。"列奥说,"我饿了,驴子,你把它分了吧,给每个人应得的那份儿。"

于是驴子把那头鹿分成了相等的三份。

"现在,我觉得每份都是同样大小的。"他说,"你想要哪份呢,列奥?"

列奥看了看那几份肉,随后他生气了。

"你这是什么意思啊,驴子!你要把这么多据为己有?"他说。

"每份都是不多不少的啊!"驴子说,"如果你不喜欢我这么分,那你就啥也别要了。"

这让列奥更加生气了,他猛地跳向驴子杀死了他。

"好了,列那,"他说,"现在只有我们两个人了,看看你能不能把这头鹿分好。"

然后,列那把所有的鹿肉都放在一堆里,只有一小块鹿腿被他单独放在了一边。

"这一大堆是你的份额,列奥。"列那说,"这一小块腿儿是我的。"

列奥对狐狸非常满意。

"列那,"他说,"是谁教会你把鹿肉分得如此恰如其分呢?"

"是死去的驴教会了我怎么分!"列那说。

9

LOBO AND THE LAMB

Lobo was hungry and thirsty.

"I wish I could find some good cold water," he said.

Soon he met Leo, the lion.

"Leo," he said, "do you know where I can get a drink?"

"Yes," said Leo, "there is a fine stream on the other side of the hill."

Lobo ran over the hill as fast as he could.

There he found the stream of clear, cold water.

"How good this is!" He said. "Now if I only had something to eat I should be happy."

He looked down the stream and there on the other side was a

九
狼和小羊

洛博又饿又渴。

"我希望我能找到一些清凉好喝的水。"他说。

没多久,他遇到了狮子列奥。

"列奥呀,"他说,"你知道我到哪儿能弄到一口喝的吗?"

"知道啊,"列奥说,"山坡那边有一条水质非常好的小溪。"

洛博以最快的速度跑过山丘。

在那里,他找到了那条小溪,溪水又清澈又冰凉。

"这水多好啊!"他说,"此刻,如果我再有一点儿东西吃,我该会多高兴啊。"

他顺着溪流往下看,对岸有一只小羊。

little lamb.

"There is my dinner," said Lobo. "Such a nice fat lamb! I must find some excuse for killing him."

So he called out in an angry voice, "how dare you make the water muddy when I want to drink it?"

"I am not making it muddy," said the lamb. "Don't you see that the water runs from you to me? See how clear and bright it is."

Lobo saw that he had made a mistake. "I must find some other way to quarrel," he said to himself.

Then he said out loud, "you are the lamb who called me names last year. Reynard told me you did."

"Reynard has told you a story," said the lamb. "I have never talked about you; and I was not born a year ago."

"Well," said the wolf, "if it was not you it must have been your father. Anyway it is all the same."

Then the wolf sprang across the stream, caught the poor lamb, and ate him up.

"这正是我的晚餐呀！"洛博说，"这么美味的一只小肥羊，我一定要找个借口杀了他！"

于是他怒声喊道："我要喝水的时候，你怎么敢把水弄浑？"

"我没把水弄浑！"小羊说，"你没有看到水是从你那边流到我这边的吗？你看它是多么清澈明亮。"

洛博意识到他犯了一个错误。"我一定要再找个吵架的借口！"他自言自语道。

于是他大声说："你就是去年骂过我的那只小羊。列那告诉我，你骂过我。"

"列那对你撒了谎！"小羊说，"我从来没有谈起过你，况且一年前我还没出生呢。"

"嗯？"狼说，"如果不是你，那一定是你的爸爸，反正都是一样的！"

接着，狼跳过小溪，抓住了可怜的小羊，把他吃掉了。

10
REYNARD AND MRS. CRANE

"I think I will play a trick on Mrs. Crane," said Reynard one day.

So he went to the pond where Mrs. Crane lived.

"Good morning, Mrs. Crane," said Reynard. "You have not been to my house for a long time. Won't you come and take dinner with me today?"

"Thank you, Reynard," said Mrs. Crane. "I shall be glad to come."

When dinner was ready, all they had to eat was soup served in a

十
狐狸和鹤

"我想我应该捉弄一下鹤夫人。"有一天列那说。

就这样,他去了鹤夫人居住的池塘。

"早上好啊,鹤夫人!"列那说,"你好久没去我家了,你今天愿意来和我一起吃顿饭吗?"

"谢谢你,列那,"鹤夫人说,"我很高兴去。"

这时,晚餐准备好了,他们要吃的东西就是盛在一个大平底盘子里的汤。

"过来吃饭吧。"列那说,"我希望你会喜欢这道好喝的热汤。"

有着长长的喙的鹤夫人从盘子里什么也吃不到。

列那用他宽大的舌头飞速地把汤都喝净了。

big flat dish.

"Come and eat," said Reynard. "I hope you will like this good hot soup."

Mrs. Crane could get nothing out of the dish with her long bill.

Reynard with his broad tongue quickly ate up all the soup.

"Why, Mrs. Crane," said Reynard, "you didn't eat anything."

"No," said Mrs. Crane, "I can't eat out of such a flat dish."

Reynard laughed at Mrs. Crane.

"That is a good joke," he said.

"I must go now," said Mrs. Crane. "Won't you come and take dinner with me tomorrow?"

"Thank you," said Reynard. "I shall be glad to."

So next day Reynard went to Mrs. Crane's home.

"Good morning, Reynard," said Mrs. Crane. "Dinner is ready. Come this way. Here is soup in this tall jar. I hope you will like it."

The jar was tall and the neck was narrow. The soup did not reach to the top. Reynard could not get a taste. Mrs. Crane ate it all with her long bill.

"How do you like my joke, Reynard?" Asked Mrs. Crane.

"哎哟，鹤夫人，"列那说，"你什么都没吃呀！"

"是呀，"鹤夫人说，"我不会从这种平底的盘子里吃东西。"

列那嘲笑起鹤夫人。

"这个玩笑太有趣了！"他说。

"现在我该走了。"鹤夫人说，"你明天愿意来和我一起吃顿饭吗？"

"谢谢你，"列那说，"我很高兴去。"

于是第二天列那就去了鹤夫人的家。

"早上好呀，列那！"鹤夫人说，"早餐准备好了，到这边来吧。这个高高的瓶子里面是汤汁，我希望你能喜欢它。"

瓶子很高，而颈部又很窄，汤汁也没有灌到顶。列那一口也没吃到，鹤夫人却用她那长长的喙把汤全都喝了。

"你觉得我这个玩笑怎么样，列那？"鹤夫人问。

11
THE DOG AND HIS SHADOW

One day Mr. Brown, the butcher, said, "are you hungry, Bruno? You look nearly starved. Here is a fine piece of meat."

Bruno was glad to get the meat. He started for home as fast as he could run. On his way he passed Reynard, the fox.

"Hello, Bruno," said Reynard. "Where did you get that nice piece of meat? Can't you stop and talk a while? It is such a long time since you came to see me. Do stop for a few minutes."

But Bruno had heard of Reynard's tricks and he only ran on faster.

On the way home he had to cross a little stream of water. He stopped on the bridge and looked down. He saw his shadow in the

十一
狗和他的影子

有一天,屠夫布朗先生说:"你饿了吗,布鲁诺?你看起来快要饿死了,这是一块上好的肉。"

布鲁诺很高兴得到了肉,他以最快的速度起身往家跑。在路上,他从狐狸列那身边经过。

"你好哇,布鲁诺!"列那说,"你从哪儿弄来这么好的一块肉啊?你就不能停下来聊一会儿吗?你已经这么久没有来看我了,真的,停下来几分钟就行。"

但布鲁诺早就听说过列那的那些鬼把戏,所以他跑得更快了。

在回家的路上,他必须要穿过一条小溪。他在桥上驻足往下看,他看到了自己在水里的影子。

water.

"Why," he said to himself, "there is another dog. He has some meat too. I believe his piece is larger than mine. Yes, I am sure it is larger. I am going to fight that dog and get his piece of meat."

So Bruno dropped his piece of meat into the water. He jumped in to fight the other dog. But there was no other dog there.

Then he tried to find his own piece of meat, but it was at the bottom of the river.

"By being so greedy I have lost my dinner," said Bruno to himself as he walked slowly home.

"啊唷!"他自言自语道,"那儿还有另一条狗耶,他也有些肉呢。我相信他的那块肉比我的还要大。没错,我可以肯定它更大!我要和那条狗打一架,然后得到他的那块肉。"

于是布鲁诺把他的那块肉丢进了水里,跳进去和另一只狗打架。但是,其实那里并没有别的狗。

然后他试图找到自己的那块肉,但是它已经沉到河底了。

"由于太过贪婪,我竟失去了晚餐……"布鲁诺一边自言自语一边慢慢地走回了家。

12
HOW THE MONKEY SETTLED THE QUARREL

Pussy and another cat once found a big piece of cheese. They began to quarrel about it.

Jocko, the monkey, passed that way. He heard them quarreling and stopped to listen.

"Why, Pussy," he said, "what is the matter?"

"I found this piece of cheese," said Pussy. "It is mine, and I am going to keep it."

"No, it is mine," said the other cat. "I saw it first."

"But I ran and picked it up first," said Pussy. "So it is mine, isn't it, Jocko?"

十二
猴子是如何解决争吵的

有一次,佩西和另一只猫发现了一大块芝士,他们开始为此争吵起来。

猴子乔科正从那儿路过,听到他们争吵就停下来去听。

"啊呀,佩西,"他说,"这是怎么回事啊?"

"我发现了这块芝士。"佩西说,"它是我的,我要留下它。"

"不,这是我的!"另一只猫说,"我先看到它的。"

"但是我先跑过去把它捡起来的。"佩西说,"所以它是我的,不是吗,乔科?"

"你们为什么不把它切成两份,然后每人拿一份呢?"猴子问道。

"这是个好主意呀!"佩西说,"我马上就切。"

"Why don't you cut it into two parts and each takes one part?" Asked the monkey.

"That is a good idea," said Pussy. "I will cut it at once."

"No, you shall not," said the other cat. "I will cut it myself."

"I will not let you cut it," said Pussy. "I know you would take the larger piece."

"Let me cut it," said the monkey. "I am sure I can cut it into two equal parts."

"That is fair," said Pussy. "I can trust you, Jocko."

"You are a good friend of mine, Jocko," said the other cat. "Cut it as quickly as you can."

So Jocko got a big knife. He cut the cheese into two pieces. Then he looked at each part.

"I think this piece is larger than the other," he said. "Yes, I know it is larger. I will bite some off this piece, so that both will be alike."

Then he took a big bite off one piece.

"Now I believe the other piece is a little larger," he said. "I will take a little off that one too."

"不，你不可以！"另一只猫说，"必须我自己来切。"

"我不愿意让你切它。"佩西说，"我知道你肯定会拿走一大块。"

"让我切吧。"猴子说，"我肯定能把它切成相等的两份。"

"这很公平！"佩西说，"我相信你，乔科。"

"你是我的好朋友，乔科！"另一只猫说，"切吧，越快越好！"

于是猴子去取了一把大刀。他把芝士切成两块，然后他看了看每一块。

"我觉得这一块比另一块更大一些。"他说，"是的，我看得出它更大一些。我应该把这块咬掉一些，这样两块就一样大了。"

然后他从这块中咬掉了一大口。

"现在我确信另一块更大一点儿。"他说，"我应该再从那块咬掉一点儿。"

"哦，乔科，"佩西叫道，"别那么做。把芝士给我们，让我们走吧。"

"不！"乔科说，"在这两块平分秋色之前，我不能把它给你们。如果我那样做，你们可能还会吵架。好了，你看

"Oh, Jocko," cried Pussy, "don't do that. Give us our cheese and let us go."

"No," said Jocko, "I will not give it to you until both parts are even. You might quarrel again if I did. Now you see this part is larger. I will fix it."

"Oh, Jocko," cried the other cat, "give us our cheese. We will not quarrel any more. Indeed, we will not."

"Just wait a moment," said the monkey.

He nibbled first from one piece and then from the other.

"Now, Jocko," said Pussy, "please give us the rest. There is not much left, but let us have it."

"What is left," said Jocko, "is just enough to pay me for settling this quarrel. You don't expect me to work for nothing, do you?"

Then he quickly ate all the cheese that was left and ran away.

"What foolish cats we are!" Said Pussy. "By quarreling we have fed the monkey while we shall have to go hungry."

"Yes," said the other cat. "We will not quarrel again."

这块更大了，我应该把它处理一下。"

"哦，乔科，"另一只猫叫道，"把奶酪给我们吧。我们不会再吵架了，真的，我们不会再吵了。"

"稍等一下。"猴子说。

他先从一块上咬下一点儿，又从另一块上咬下一点儿来。

"好了吧，乔科，"佩西说，"请把剩下的给我们吧。剩下的不多了，让我们把它吃了吧。"

"剩下的嘛……"猴子说，"刚刚够付给我解决你们这场争吵的报酬。你们不会指望我白白干活吧，是不是？"

接着，他飞速地吃掉了剩下的所有奶酪，然后跑掉了。

"我们真是愚蠢的猫啊！"佩西说，"只顾争吵，把猴子喂饱了，而我们自己却不得不挨饿。"

"是啊，"另一只猫说，"我们再也不会吵架了。"

13
THE WOLF AND THE SHEEP

Some dogs chased Lobo one day. One of them bit him in the neck. Lobo turned to fight him when another bit his leg. A third bit his side.

"I can't fight so many," said Lobo.

So he ran to the woods as fast as he could. The dogs could not follow him there.

Lobo lay down under some bushes. The blood ran from his side and legs. He was weak and faint. He stayed there for three days.

"What shall I do?" He asked. "I am too weak to hunt for food. I shall die unless I can get something to eat. If some animal would only come near me, I might catch it."

十三
狼和绵羊

一天,几只狗追捕狼洛博,其中一只狗咬了他的脖子。当洛博转身与他搏斗时,另一只狗咬了他的腿;第三只咬了他的肋部。

"我可打不过这么多狗啊!"洛博说。

所以他以最快的速度跑向树林,狗没法追到那里。

洛博躺在几簇灌木丛下,鲜血从他的肋部和腿上流了下来。他虚弱又无力,在那里躺了三天。

"我该怎么办呢?"他说,"我太虚弱了,无法打猎找食。除非我能找到吃的东西,否则我会死的。只要有什么动物走近我,我就有可能捉住它。"

不久,一只绵羊到这边来找草吃。

Soon a sheep came that way looking for grass.

"Oh, Sheep," cried Lobo, "where are you going?"

"I am going over to the other hill," said the sheep. "The grass there is fresh and green."

"I am sick," said Lobo. "Won't you stop and do something for me first?"

"What do you want?" said the sheep.

"I am hungry and thirsty," said Lobo. "The dogs bit my legs so that I cannot walk. If you will only bring me a drink I am sure I can find some meat."

"No, I will not," said the sheep. "If I go near enough to give you a drink, you will use me for meat."

"哦,绵羊,"洛博叫道,"你要去哪里呀?"

"我要去那边的山坡上,"绵羊说,"那里的草又鲜又绿。"

"我病了。"洛博说,"你能不能先停下来为我做点儿什么呢?"

"需要我做什么呢?"绵羊说。

"我是又饿又渴啊!"洛博说,"那些狗咬了我的大腿,所以我无法走路。只要你能拿点儿水给我,我相信,我还是能找到肉吃的。"

"不,我不愿意!"绵羊说,"如果我送水给你,就得离你很近,我就会成了你要吃的肉!"

14

THE CAT AND THE MICE

The city mouse lived with her brothers and sisters in a fine big house.

A cat lived there too. Everyday she hunted for mice. Nearly everyday she caught one or two.

"What shall we do?" Cried one mouse. "She will soon eat all of us."

One night the mice had a meeting to talk about the dreadful cat. Each mouse told how the cat had frightened him.

One mouse said, "if I go to the pantry to get a bit of cheese, she jumps at me."

Another said, "if I go to the kitchen for a little piece of bread, I

十四
猫和老鼠们

城里的老鼠和她的兄弟姐妹住在一个漂亮的大房子里。

一只猫也住在那里。她每天都在猎杀老鼠,她几乎每天都要抓到一两只。

"我们该怎么办呀?"一只老鼠叫道,"她很快就会把我们全都吃光了啊。"

一天晚上,老鼠们开会议论那只可怕的猫,每只老鼠都述说了猫是如何吓到自己的。

一只老鼠说:"要是我去食品储藏室取一点儿奶酪,她就会向我跳过来。"

另一个说:"要是我去厨房取一小块面包,我可以看到她明亮的眼睛在黑暗中闪闪发光。"

can see her bright eyes shining in the dark."

A little mouse said, "last week I went to the dining room to pick up a few crumbs. She chased me and nearly caught me. I was so frightened that I have not dared to go out of my hole since."

"We must do something," said an old mouse.

"Let us all together run at her and bite her," said one mouse.

"No," said another mouse, "that will not do. We cannot frighten her."

"Listen to me," said a young mouse. "I have a fine plan. You know the cat walks so softly that we can never hear her coming. Let us tie a bell around her neck. When she walks the bell will ring. Then we can hear it and run away."

"Good, good!" Cried the mice. "What a fine play! Let us get a bell at once."

"Wait a minute," cried an old mouse. "Which of you is going to tie the bell on the cat?"

一只小老鼠说:"上周我去餐厅拾几块面包屑,她就追着我,还差点儿抓住我。我吓坏了,从那以后就再也不敢出洞了。"

"我们一定要做点儿什么。"一只年岁大的老鼠说。

"让我们大家一起袭击她,咬她。"一只小老鼠说。

"不!"另一只说,"那不行,我们吓唬不住她。"

"听我说,"一只小老鼠说,"我倒是有一个好办法。你们知道猫走路很轻,我们总是听不到她什么时候来。让我们在她的脖子上系一个铃铛,当她走路时,铃声就会响起来。那样咱们听见了,就能跑掉了。"

"好哇,好哇!"老鼠们叫了起来,"这真是个妙招啊!让我们赶紧把铃铛拿来吧。"

"等一下,"一只年长的老鼠喊道,"你们哪一个去把铃铛系在猫身上呢?"

15

REYNARD IN THE WELL

One day as Reynard was going through a field he fell into a well. There was not much water in the well but he could not get out. He called for help as loud as he could.

"I don't see how I can ever get out of this unless someone comes to help me," he said.

He called again and again.

After a long time, Lobo, the wolf, passed that way. He stopped to listen.

"I think I hear someone calling," he said to himself. "It sounds like that fox, Reynard. I wonder where he is."

Then he saw the well and looked in. Away down at the bottom

十五
井里的狐狸

一天，当狐狸列那穿过一片田野时，他掉进了一口井里。井里没有多少水，但他出不来，他尽可能大声地呼救。

"我弄不清楚究竟怎样才能从这里逃出去，除非有人来帮助我。"他说。

他一遍又一遍地呼救。

过了很久，狼洛博路过那里，他驻足听了听。

"我想我听到了有人在呼唤。"他自言自语道，"听起来像是那只狐狸列那。我想知道他在哪儿呢？"

这时他看到了那口井，便往里看。在井底下，他看到了列那。

"啊唷，列那，"他说，"是你吗？"

he saw Reynard.

"Why, Reynard," he said, "is that you?"

"Yes, it is me," said Reynard. "I am so glad to see you, Lobo. I know you will help me out."

"How did you get down there, Reynard?" Asked Lobo. "I should think you would be very cold."

"I fell in," said Reynard. "I was running and I did not see the well. Please help me out. Then I will tell you all about it."

"Poor little Reynard!" Said Lobo. "Your fur is all wet, too. I am afraid you will be sick."

"Won't you please help me now, Lobo? I am so cold," said Reynard, beginning to cry.

"I am so sorry for you, Reynard," said Lobo. "I am afraid you will starve if you don't get out soon. How dreadful it would be if you were to die!"

"Oh, Wolf," said Reynard, "don't talk so much. Help me out first and then pity me afterward."

But Lobo only laughed and ran away.

Reynard called and called after him, but he did not come back.

"是的,是我,"列那说,"我真高兴见到你,洛博。我知道你会帮我出去的。"

"你是怎么掉到那儿去的,列那?"洛博问道,"我想你一定很冷吧。"

"我是跌进来的。"列那说,"我正在奔跑,没有看到井。请救我出去吧,到那时我会把一切都告诉你的。"

"可怜的小列那!"洛博说,"你的皮毛也都湿了吧,我担心你可能会生病的。"

"您现在能不能帮帮我,洛博?我好冷啊。"列那说着,便开始哭了起来。

"我真为你感到难过呀,列那。"洛博说,"我担心如果你再不快点儿出来的话,可能就饿死了。如果你要是死了,那该会多么可怕啊!"

"哦,狼啊,"列那说,"别说那么多了。先救我出去,然后再怜悯我吧。"

但洛博只是笑了笑就跑开了。

列那在他身后叫了又叫,但是,他没有回来。

过了一会儿,山羊听到列那在呼叫,便走到井边往里看。

当看到狐狸时,他说:"啊唷,列那,你在那下面做什

After a while, the goat heard Reynard calling. He went to the well and looked in.

When he saw the fox he said, "why, Reynard, what are you doing down there?"

"I shall not tell him that I am in trouble," said Reynard to himself.

Then he said out loud, "oh, I just came down here to get a drink. It is so nice and cool and the water is so good that I like to stay here."

"I am very thirsty," said the goat. "I wish I had some water."

"Come down," said Reynard. "There is plenty for both of us."

"How can I get down?" Asked the goat.

"Jump and I will catch you," said Reynard.

So the goat jumped into the well with the fox and drank all the water he could.

"Isn't this fine water?" Asked Reynard.

"Yes, the best I ever tasted. Now how do we get out?"

"That is easy," said Reynard. "First, put your forefeet up against the side of the well as high as you can reach. That is the way. Then

么呀？"

"我不会告诉他我有麻烦了。"列那自言自语道。

于是他冲着外边大声说："哦，我只是到这下边来喝口水。这里非常宜人，非常凉爽；正是这里的水非常好喝，我才喜欢待在这里。"

"我正很渴呢，"山羊说，"我希望我也能喝点儿水。"

"那就下来吧，"列那说，"这里有足够的水满足我们俩喝。"

"我怎么能下去呢？"山羊问道。

"往下跳，我会接住你的。"列那说。

于是山羊跳进井里和狐狸待在了一起，随后他喝足了水。

"这水是不是很好喝呀？"列那问道。

"是的，这是我尝过的最好的水了。现在我们怎么出去呢？"

"这很容易的。"列那说，"首先，把你的前脚踩在井壁上，够得越高越好，就是这样的。然后我踩着你的肩膀，再踩着你的头，然后就跳出去了，就像这样。现在我出来了，非常感谢你，比利。"

然后列那走开了，把可怜的山羊留在了井里。

"列那，列那！"他叫道，"回来帮我出去。"

"我可没时间哪，"列那说，"时候不早了，我该回家了。

I step on your shoulders and on your head and jump out. Like this. Now I am out. Thank you very much, Billy."

Then Reynard walked away and left the poor goat in the well.

"Reynard, Reynard," he called, "come back and help me out."

"I haven't time," said Reynard. "It is getting late, and I must go home. But let me tell you something: if you had been wise you would have looked before you leaped."

但让我告诉你一件事：如果你是明智的，你会在跳下去之前留点儿神。"

16

THE WOLF AND THE CRANE

Lobo, the wolf, went hunting and caught a fat duck. He was hungry and he ate it so fast that a bone stuck in his throat.

"Oh, what shall I do?" Cried Lobo. "I cannot get it out. I am afraid I shall choke to death."

Just then he saw Reynard, the fox, running across a field.

"Oh, Reynard," he called, "please come here. I have a bone in my throat. I am afraid I shall choke to death. Please help me get it out."

"I won't do it," said Reynard. "You would not help me out of the well yesterday. I won't help you now."

Then Lobo saw Bunny, the hare.

十六
狼和鹤

狼洛博去打猎,他抓到了一只肥肥的鸭子。他饿了,吃得太快了,喉咙里卡了一根骨头。

"哦,我该怎么办哪?"洛博叫道,"我没办法把它拿出来,我担心我会被噎死的。"

就在这时,他看到了狐狸列那,他正在田野上奔跑。

"哦,列那,"他喊道,"请到这里来一下吧!我的喉咙里卡了一根骨头,我担心我会窒息而死的,请帮我把它弄出来吧。"

"我不会这样做的!"列那说,"你昨天都不愿意帮我从井里出来,我现在也没必要帮助你。"

这时洛博看到了野兔邦尼。

"邦尼,邦尼!"他叫道,"请帮帮我吧,我的喉咙里卡

"Bunny, Bunny," he called, "please help me. I have a bone in my throat. I am afraid I shall choke to death."

"That is too bad," said Bunny. "Open your mouth and let me see. Yes, I can see it but, Lobo, I cannot reach it. I will tell you what to do. Go down to the lake and call Mrs. Crane. She has such a long bill, that I am sure she can get it out."

So Lobo went down to the lake where Mrs. Crane lived.

She was out in the water trying to catch some frogs.

"Dear Mrs. Crane," Lobo called, "won't you come here? I want you to help me."

了一根骨头，我担心我会窒息而死的。"

"那太糟糕了！"邦尼说，"张开你的嘴，让我看看。是的，我可以看到它；但是，洛博，我够不到它。不过，我愿意告诉你该怎么做。你到湖边去拜访一下鹤夫人，她有那么长的喙，我可以肯定，她能把它取出来。"

所以洛博就向鹤夫人居住的湖边走去。

她正站在水里，打算抓些青蛙。

"亲爱的鹤夫人，"洛博叫道，"您能到这儿来一下吗？我需要您帮帮我。"

"不，我不能去！"鹤夫人说，"你杀死了我的一个兄弟，我知道你还想捉住我。"

"请帮帮我吧！"洛博乞求道，"真的，我不会伤害您的。我的喉咙里卡了一根骨头，我没法把它拿出来。您有这么优美颀长的喙，您肯定可以把它拔出来。一定要过来试试好吗？如果您愿意做，我会付给您丰厚报酬的。"

就这样，鹤夫人从湖里出来了。

这时洛博张大了嘴巴，鹤夫人向喉咙里看。

"我看见了！"她说，"好了，别动，洛博。"

她把头伸进洛博的嘴里，她长长的喙叼住那块骨头，一

"No, I will not," Mrs. Crane said. "You killed one of my brothers and I know you want to catch me, too."

"Please help me," begged Lobo. "Indeed, I will not hurt you. I have a bone in my throat and I cannot get it out. You have such a nice long bill, I am sure you could pull it out. Do come and try. I will pay you well if you will."

So Mrs. Crane came out of the lake.

Then Lobo opened his mouth very wide and Mrs. Crane looked down his throat.

"I see it," she said. "Now hold still, Lobo."

She put her head into Lobo's mouth. Her long bill caught hold of the bone, and it was out in a minute.

"Here it is, Lobo," said Mrs. Crane. "Now give me my money and I will go."

"I will not give you anything," said Lobo. "Wasn't it pay enough that I did not bite your head off when I had it in my mouth? What more do you want?"

下子就把骨头叼了出来。

"给你看看吧,洛博。"鹤夫人说,"好了,把钱给我吧,我该走了。"

"我不会给你任何东西的!"洛博说,"你的头在我嘴里时,我没有咬掉它,难道这个报酬还不够吗?你还想要什么?"

17
THE ANT AND THE GRASSHOPPER

A grasshopper met an ant in the field one day.

"Why do you work so hard, Mrs. Ant?" Asked the grasshopper. "Come over here and play with me."

"I cannot play with you, Grasshopper," said the ant. "I am putting away food for winter. Don't you do any work?"

"Oh, I don't like to work," said the grasshopper. "It is more fun to jump and sing."

"But winter is coming," said the ant.

"What is the use of thinking about winter?" Asked the grasshopper. "There is plenty of food now, and I want to have a good time."

"You may be sorry some day," said the ant. "I haven't time to

十七
蚂蚁和蚱蜢

有一天，一只蚱蜢在田野里遇到了一只蚂蚁。

"你为什么这么辛苦地劳作啊，蚂蚁太太？"蚱蜢问道，"过来陪我玩玩吧。"

"我不能陪你一起玩呀，蚱蜢。"蚂蚁说，"我正在储存冬天的食物，你不干点儿什么活儿吗？"

"哦，我不喜欢干活儿！"蚱蜢说，"跳跳唱唱的多有乐趣啊！"

"但是冬天快到了啊。"蚂蚁说。

"考虑冬天有什么用啊？"蚱蜢问道，"现在有很多食物，我想玩得开心。"

"总有一天你会后悔的！"蚂蚁说，"我没有时间再和你

talk to you any longer. Goodbye."

The cold days came. The ground was hard, and everything was covered with snow.

The grasshopper could find nothing to eat. At last he went to the ants' house.

"Dear ants," he said, "won't you please give me something to eat? I am so cold and hungry."

"Why have you no food of your own?" Asked a big ant. "Why didn't you save some grain and leaves last summer?"

"Oh," said the grasshopper, "I was so happy last summer; I could not work. It was so warm and bright that I sang and danced all day."

"Well," said the ants, "if you danced all summer you will have to starve all winter."

唠嗑了,再见。"

寒冷的日子来了,大地坚硬,一切都被雪覆盖了。

蚱蜢找不到任何东西吃,最后,他去了蚂蚁们的家里。

"亲爱的蚂蚁,"他说,"你愿意给我点儿吃的东西吗?我好冷好饿呀。"

"你为什么没有自己的食物呢?"一只大蚂蚁问道,"去年夏天你为什么不储存点儿谷物和树叶呢?"

"哦,"蚱蜢说,"上个夏天我光顾快活了,没能顾上干活儿。天气是那么温暖明亮,我整天只顾唱歌跳舞了。"

"唉!"蚂蚁们说,"要是你整个夏天都只顾跳舞,那你整个冬天必然得挨饿了。"

18

THE COUNTRY MOUSE AND THE CITY MOUSE

A mouse had a nice little home in the country. Her cousin lived in a big house in the city.

One day the city mouse came to visit her.

"Good morning," she said. "I have come a long way to see you. I was afraid I might not find you at home so I came early."

"I am very glad to see you," said the country mouse. "Sit down and rest while I get dinner. Here are beans and peas and some grains of wheat. Do come and eat."

"Poor thing!" Thought the city mouse. "How little she has to eat! I should think she would starve; but I must not let her see that I

十八
乡下老鼠和城里老鼠

一只老鼠在乡下有一个不错的小房子,她的表姐住在城里的一所大房子里。

有一天,城里的老鼠来看她。

"早上好啊!"她说,"走了好长一段路过来看你,我担心在家里有可能找不到你,所以我就早早过来了。"

"见到你我太高兴了!"乡下老鼠说,"坐下来休息一下吧,我去准备饭。这里有菜豆、豌豆还有一些小麦粒,快来吃点儿呀。"

"这什么破东西呀!"城里老鼠心里想,"她的吃食也太少了!我想她可能会饿死的;不过,我不能让她看出来我在为她感到难过。"

am sorry for her."

Then she said out loud, "you are very kind. I did not have any breakfast this morning. I am very hungry."

And she politely nibbled a few peas and ate some wheat.

When they had finished, the city mouse said, "don't you get very lonesome out here in the country?"

"No," said the country mouse, "I like it here."

"But it is so quiet," said the city mouse. "In the city there is so much to see and do."

"It must be very wonderful there," said the country mouse.

于是她大声说:"你真是太好了,我今天早上一点儿早餐都没吃,我正很饿呢。"

然后她礼貌性地啃了几颗豌豆并吃了一些小麦粒。

等她们吃完了饭,城里老鼠说:"你在这乡下野外不感到非常寂寞吗?"

"不!"乡下老鼠说,"我喜欢这里呀。"

"可是这里太僻静了。"城里老鼠说,"在城里,我们有很多可看的和可做的事。"

"城里那儿一定很美妙吧。"乡下老鼠说,"请给我讲一讲吧。"

"我和姐妹们住在一个很大的房子里,"城里老鼠说,"有好多房间,而且我们有非常美味的东西可吃。"

"都有什么东西呀?"乡下老鼠问道。

"哦,有点心、馅饼、奶酪和火鸡,以及你能想到的所有好吃的东西。"城里老鼠答道。

"真希望我也能吃到这些东西,"乡下老鼠说,"我还从来没尝过馅饼和点心的味道呢。"

"跟我回家吧,"城里老鼠说,"我会把你能吃到的好东西都给你。"

"Please tell me about it."

"My sisters and I live in a very large house," said the city mouse. "There are many rooms, and we have such fine things to eat."

"What kind of things?" Asked the country mouse.

"Oh, cake and pie and cheese and turkey, and everything good that you can think of," replied the city mouse.

"I wish I could have some of them," said the country mouse. "I have never tasted pie or cake."

"Come home with me," said the city mouse. "I will give you all the good things you can eat."

"I wish I might go," said the country mouse.

"Go with me tonight," said the city mouse. "There is plenty of room where I live. After you have been there a few days you will never want to come back here."

"All right," said the country mouse. "I will go."

"We will start as soon as it is dark," said the city mouse. "Then no one can see us."

So as soon as it was dark, the country mouse and her cousin started for the city. They ran and ran until the country mouse was

"我要是能去最好了。"乡下老鼠说。

"今晚就跟我走吧。"城里老鼠说,"我们住的地方有充裕的房间。你在那里住过几天后,肯定再也不愿意回到这里了。"

"好吧,"乡下老鼠说,"我愿意去。"

"我们天一黑就得出发。"城里老鼠说,"那样,就没有人能看到我们了。"

就这样,天刚一黑,乡下老鼠和她的表姐就出发奔向城里。她们跑了一程又一程,直到乡下老鼠跑累了。

"表姐,"她说,"我们停在这儿歇一歇吧,我太累了,我一步都跑不动了。"

"哦,快点儿吧!"城里老鼠说,"没多远了,想一想我们就要吃到的美味晚餐吧。"

因此她们又继续跑。

"这里是房子。"城里老鼠说,"现在跟着我,我领你看那个洞,我们从那里进去。现在我们进来了。看呀!这是不是一个漂亮的地方呀?"

"是,"乡下老鼠说,"它很漂亮。好了,好吃的东西在哪儿呢?"

"它们在储藏室里。"城里老鼠说,"往这边来。好了,你

tired.

"Cousin," she said, "let us stop here and rest. I am so tired that I cannot run another step."

"Oh, come on," said the city mouse. "It is not much farther. Think of the good supper we shall have."

So they ran on again.

"Here is the house," said the city mouse. "Now follow me and I will show you the hole where we get in. Now we are in. Look! Isn't this a fine place?"

"Yes," said the country mouse, "it is beautiful. Now where are the good things to eat?"

"They are in the pantry," said the city mouse. "Come this way. Now, can't you smell them? Slip through this hole and then you shall have all you want."

"Is this big place the pantry?" Asked the country mouse.

"Yes;now jump up on this shelf. Here are the cakes. Over there are the pies. Just try some of this crust. Isn't it good?"

"Yes, indeed," she said. "Oh, Cousin, I am so glad I came home with you!I want to stay here always."

没闻到它们吗？悄悄地从这个洞溜过去，然后你就会得到你想要的一切。"

"这个大屋子就是储藏室吗？"乡下老鼠问道。

"是的，赶紧跳到这个架子上。这里是点心，那边是馅饼。请品尝一下这个面包皮，是不是很好吃啊？"

"是的，真好吃。"她说，"哦，表姐，我和你一起回家太高兴了！我想永远待在这里。"

就在这时，门开了。

"快跑！"城里老鼠说，"跑到洞里去。"

两只老鼠都以最快的速度跑进了洞里。

Just then the door opened.

"Run," said the city mouse. "Get back into the hole."

Both the mice ran into the hole as fast as they could.

"What was that?" Asked the country mouse. "Oh, I was so frightened!"

"That was only the cook," said the city mouse. "She will leave in a minute. Then we can go out and get some more to eat. She has gone now. Come, I smell some cheese."

They were soon back on the shelf, trying the meat and cheese.

Suddenly the door opened again and they heard a loud bark.

Again the mice ran for their hole.

"Oh, Cousin," cried the country mouse, "what dreadful thing was that?"

"That was only the dog," said the city mouse. "He won't stay long. Then we can go back again. But what is the matter?"

"I am going home, Cousin," said the country mouse. "You may have your pies and cakes and be frightened all the time if you want to. I would rather have my beans and corn in a quiet place. Goodbye."

"那是什么呀？"乡下老鼠问道，"哦，我太害怕了！"

"那不过是厨师。"城里老鼠说，"她马上就会走的，接着我们就能出去拿到更多吃的。她现在已经走了，来吧，我闻到了奶酪的味道。"

她们很快就回到了货架上，品尝着肉和奶酪。

突然，门又开了，她们听到了一声响亮的吼叫。

老鼠又跑向了她们的洞。

"哦，表姐，"乡下老鼠喊道，"那是什么可怕的东西啊？"

"那不过是只狗。"城里老鼠说，"他不会待太久的，到时候我们可以再回去的。可是，你这是怎么了呀？"

"我要回家，表姐。"乡下老鼠说，"确实，你这里又有馅饼又有点心。可要吃到它们，你得一直提心吊胆的，所以我还是安安静静地吃我的谷粒和豆子吧。再见。"

19

THE CROW AND THE PITCHER

"I wish I could find a drink," said Mrs. Crow one afternoon. "I haven't had any water since morning."

"I know where you can get some," said Bunny, the hare.

"Do tell me," said Mrs. Crow. "I am so thirsty."

"Do you see that tree over there?" Asked Bunny.

"Yes," said Mrs. Crow, "I see it."

"By the side of it is a big pitcher of water," said the hare.

"Thank you, Bunny; you are very good," said Mrs. Crow. "I will go at once."

She flew quickly to the tree.

"Yes, here is the pitcher," she said. "Now I shall have a good

十九
乌鸦和大水罐

"我多么希望能找到一口喝的呀!"一天下午,乌鸦太太说,"我从早上到现在没有喝到一点儿水。"

"我知道你在哪儿会得到一些喝的。"野兔邦尼说。

"快告诉我吧!"乌鸦太太说,"我好渴啊。"

"你看到那边的那棵树了吗?"邦尼问道。

"是的,"乌鸦太太说,"我看到了呀。"

"树的旁边就是一个盛水的大水罐。"邦尼说。

"谢谢你,邦尼,你心眼真好啊!"乌鸦太太说,"我马上就去。"

她快速地飞向那棵树。

"是的,大水罐在这儿呢。"她说,"现在我要好好喝一顿。"

drink."

The pitcher was tall, and there was not much water in it.

Mrs. Crow tried to drink, but her bill could not reach the water.

She tried first on one side of the pitcher and then on the other. She could not wet even the tip of her bill.

"What shall I do?" Said Mrs. Crow. "I must have a drink."

She stood still and thought for a minute.

"Perhaps I can break the pitcher," she said. "Then I can get a drink as the water runs out."

She pecked it with her bill, and she hit it with her foot.

"No, it is too hard," she said. "I cannot break it. I wonder if I could tip it over."

She pushed against the pitcher, but she could not move it.

"What a heavy pitcher!" She said.

She stopped and thought again.

"I will try another plan," she said.

Near the pitcher was a number of little pebbles. She picked up one in her bill and dropped it into the pitcher.

大水罐很高,而且里面并没有太多的水。

乌鸦太太尝试去喝水,但她的喙够不到水。

她先在大水罐的一侧试了试,然后又到另一侧试了试;可是,就连她的喙尖都沾不到水。

"我该怎么办呢?"乌鸦太太说,"我一定要喝水的呀。"

她一动不动地站着,想了一会儿。

"或许我可以打碎大水罐,"她说,"然后我可以在水流出来的时候喝到水。"

她用嘴啄它,又用脚踢它。

"不行啊,它太坚硬了!"她说,"我打不碎它。我想知道我是不是可以把它弄倒。"

她推挤大水罐,但搬不动它。

"好重的大水罐啊!"她说。

她停了下来,再次陷入了沉思。

Then she dropped another in. After many pebbles were dropped in, the water reached nearly to the top, and Mrs. Crow had a drink.

"Where there's a will there's a way," she said as she flew off.

"我必须尝试一下别的方法。"她说。

在大水罐附近有一些小鹅卵石。她用喙叼起一块,然后把它投进大水罐里。

接着她又投了另一块进去。在好多好多的鹅卵石被投进去之后,水差不多升到了顶部,乌鸦太太喝到了水。

"有志者事竟成。"她飞走时说。

20
REYNARD AND PUSSY

Reynard met Pussy in the forest one day.

"Do you know any tricks, Pussy?" Asked Reynard.

"I know one or two," said Pussy.

"Only one or two?" Asked Reynard. "That is not very many."

"But they are very good ones," said Pussy. "How many tricks do you know, Reynard?"

"Oh, I know a thousand," said Reynard. "I know more tricks than any animal in the forest. I know a hundred tricks to play on dogs. What would you do, Pussy, if the dogs were to come?"

"I should have but one plan," said Pussy. "If that did not help me, I should be caught."

二十
狐狸和小猫

一天，狐狸列那在森林里遇到了小猫佩西。

"你会变戏法吗，佩西？"列那问道。

"我会一两个吧。"佩西说。

"只有一两个？"列那问道，"那真不是很多啊。"

"那可是特棒的一两个！"佩西说，"你会变多少戏法呀，列那？"

"哦，我会上千个！"列那说，"我懂得的戏法比森林里的任何动物都要多。就说对付狗吧，我就有上百条妙计。如果狗要是来了，佩西，你会怎么做？"

"我可能只有一种办法。"佩西说，"如果它不管用，我就会被捉住的。"

"Poor Pussy," said Reynard. "I am sorry for you. I will teach you a few of my tricks, if you want me to."

"Listen," said Pussy. "I think I hear the dogs. There they come, Reynard. I will try my one trick."

Pussy ran up a tree and sat down on one of the branches. The dogs barked at her, but they could not reach her.

"Now I will see Reynard play some of his tricks," said Pussy.

But the fox with his many tricks could not get out of sight. The dogs chased him and bit him.

Pussy watched from the tree.

"One good plan is worth a hundred little tricks," she said.

"可怜的小猫咪，"列那说，"我真为你感到难过啊。如果你想学的话，我可以教你几招。"

"你听啊！"佩西说，"我想我听到了狗的动静。他们来了，列那，我必须试一下我的一个戏法。"

佩西跑到一棵树上，坐在一根树枝上。狗对着她大声吼叫，但他们却够不到她。

"现在，我倒想看看列那玩他的把戏。"佩西说。

但狐狸徒有一身妙计却难以脱身。狗群向他追赶过去，咬住了他。

佩西远远地在树上注视着。

"一个良策胜过百条妙计！"她说。

21
LOBO AND BRUNO

One day Bruno met Lobo, the wolf, in the woods.

"Why, Lobo," he said, "what is the matter? You are so thin, I hardly knew you."

"I am nearly starved, Bruno," said Lobo. "I haven't had anything to eat for a long time."

"Can't you catch anything?" Asked Bruno.

"No," said Lobo. "I have hunted and hunted, but I can't find even a mouse. How fat you are, Bruno! You must have a great deal to eat."

"Oh, yes," said Bruno. "I have all that I want."

"Where do you get it?" Asked Lobo.

二十一
狼和狗

有一天，狗布鲁诺在树林里遇到了狼洛博。

"啊唷，洛博，"他说，"这是怎么回事哎？你也太瘦了吧，我都快认不出你了。"

"我快要饿死了，布鲁诺。"洛博说，"我已经好久没吃任何东西了。"

"你什么东西都抓不到吗？"布鲁诺问道。

"是啊，"洛博说，"我一次又一次出去捕猎，可是，我甚至连一只老鼠都找不到。看你有多胖啊，布鲁诺！你一定有很多很多的东西吃吧。"

"哦，是的，"布鲁诺说，"我能吃到我想要的一切东西。"

"那你从哪里弄来的呢？"洛博问道。

"My master gives it to me."

"Does he give you meat?"

"Yes, I have meat three times each day. Sometimes there is so much that I cannot eat it all. Then I take what is left and bury it. My master is very good to me. He plays with me and pets me everyday."

"I wish I had such a home," said Lobo.

"Come home with me," said Bruno. "You can live with me and help me guard the house at night."

"That will be fine," said Lobo. "Let us go at once."

"是我主人给我的。"

"他给你肉吃吗?"

"是的,我每天会有三顿肉。有时候肉太多了,我不能全部吃掉,那么我就会把剩下的肉埋起来。我主人对我很友善,他每天都和我一起玩耍,还抚摸我。"

"我要是有这样一个家该有多好啊!"洛博说。

"跟我回家吧。"布鲁诺说,"你可以和我住在一起,晚上帮我看守房子。"

"那可太好了!"洛博说,"我们马上走吧。"

于是布鲁诺和洛博一起沿着马路奔跑过去。

他们还没走多远,这时,洛博说:"等一下,布鲁诺,你脖子边上的那个疤痕是怎么回事?"

"那不算什么,"布鲁诺说,"是链子把皮毛擦掉了一小块。"

"什么链子?"洛博问道。

"他们用来把我拴上的那个啊。"布鲁诺说。

"他们用链子把你拴起来吗?"洛博问道。

"呃,对呀!"布鲁诺说,"所有的狗有时都会用链子拴住呀。"

"他们也会把我拴住吗?"洛博问道。

So Bruno and Lobo ran down the road together.

They had not gone far when Lobo said, "wait a minute, Bruno. What is that mark on the side of your neck?"

"That isn't anything," said Bruno. "The chain rubbed the hair off a little bit."

"What chain?" Asked Lobo.

"The one they fasten me with," said Bruno.

"Do they fasten you with a chain?" Asked Lobo.

"Why, yes," said Bruno, "all dogs are fastened with chains, sometimes."

"Would they fasten me, too?" Asked Lobo.

"Yes," said Bruno, "I think they would, once in a while."

"I won't be fastened with a chain," said Lobo. "I am going back to the woods. I would rather be free, even if I do not get much to eat, than to have three meals each day and be fastened with a chain."

"是的,"布鲁诺说,"我想他们偶尔会这样做的吧。"

"我才不乐意被链子拴住哪!"洛博说,"我要回到树林里去了。比起被链子拴着每天吃上三顿饭,我更愿意自由自在,虽然我可能弄不到多少吃的。"

22
THE QUARREL

"Where are you going, Leo?" Asked Bruin one morning.

"I am going hunting," said Leo. "I haven't had anything to eat for two days."

"Let me go with you," said Bruin. "I think I know where we can catch a deer."

"I am very fond of fat deer," said Leo. "Which way shall we go?"

"Let us go up on the mountain," said Bruin. "I caught some sheep there last week."

So Leo and Bruin started off together.

For a long time they hunted, but could not find anything. At

二十二
争吵

"你要去哪里啊,列奥?"一天早上,布鲁因问道。

"我要去打猎。"列奥说,"我已经两天没吃东西了。"

"让我和你一起去吧。"布鲁因说,"我想我知道我们在哪里可以抓到鹿。"

"我最喜欢肥美的鹿了!"列奥说,"我们应该走哪条路呢?"

"我们爬上这座山吧,"布鲁因说,"上周我在那边抓到了羊。"

于是,列奥和布鲁因一起出发了。

他们打了很长时间猎,但是没有找到任何东西。终于,他们看到了一只小鹿,他们两个一跃而上杀死了它。

鹿很小,而列奥和布鲁因两个都饿了。

last they saw a little deer. They both sprang upon it and killed it.

The deer was small, and Leo and Bruin were both hungry.

"There is not enough for both of us," said Leo. "You go and catch something else, Bruin. I want all of this deer myself."

"You shall not have it," said Bruin. "I brought you up here and showed you where to find it. It is mine."

"No, it is not," said Leo. "I killed it with my strong jaws."

"No, I killed it with my big paws," said Bruin.

Then they began to fight. Leo bit Bruin, and Bruin hit Leo. Leo roared. And Bruin growled.

Reynard, the fox, was also hunting on the mountain that morning. He heard the noise and came to see what was the matter.

"Why, Bruin and Leo are fighting," he said. "I will watch them a while. I will hide behind this bush so they cannot see me."

So he sat down and watched them a long time.

"I wonder what they are fighting about," Reynard said to himself. "I think I will creep up a little nearer and see."

Then he hid behind a big rock that was near.

"Oh, yes, I see," said he. "They have killed a little deer and

"这也不够我们俩吃啊!"列奥说,"你去捉点儿别的东西吃吧,布鲁因,我想自己一个人吃这一整头鹿。"

"你不可以吃它!"布鲁因说,"是我把你带到这里,指给你看在哪儿可以找到鹿的,它是我的。"

"不,不是你的!"列奥说,"是我用强有力的下颚咬死了它。"

"不,是我用我的一对大爪子杀死了它!"布鲁因说。

接着他们打了起来。列奥咬向布鲁因,而布鲁因猛击列奥;列奥咆哮着,而布鲁因也怒吼起来。

那天早上,狐狸列那也在山上打猎。他听到了嘈杂声,就走过来看一看这是怎么回事。

"啊唷,布鲁因和列奥正在打架!"他说,"我要观察他们一会儿。我要躲在这灌木丛后面,这样他们就看不到我了。"

就这样,他坐了下来并观察了他们很久。

"我想知道他们为了什么打起来了。"列那自言自语道,"我想我必须爬得更近一点儿看看。"

于是他就躲在一块近在咫尺的大石头后面。

"哦,说真的,我明白了。"他说,"他们杀死了一只小鹿,而且两个人都想得到它。我想那头鹿可能会为我带来一

both want it. I think that deer would make a good dinner for me. I will wait a while."

Leo and Bruin still fought. At last they became so tired and worn out that they could fight no longer. They lay upon the ground and glared at each other.

"Now is my time," said Reynard. He slipped up quietly, seized the deer and ran away with it.

The lion and the bear saw him and tried to chase him, but they were too tired to go far.

They lay down again and watched Reynard. Over on the other hill he was having a fine dinner.

"How foolish we are," said the lion, "to take all this trouble to feed the fox!"

顿充足的晚餐,我情愿等一会儿。"

列奥和布鲁因还在厮打。最后,他们累得如此疲惫不堪,以至于他们再也打不动了。他们躺在地上,彼此怒目而视。

"现在,该我出场了。"列那说。他悄悄地溜了过去,夺过来那头鹿,拖着它跑掉了。

狮子和熊看见了他,并试图去追赶他;但他们太累了,已经跑不动了。

他们再一次躺下来注视着列那。在对面的那座山上,狐狸正在吃一顿美味的晚餐。

"我们真是太愚蠢了!"狮子说,"费了这么大劲,结果竟喂了狐狸!"

23

THE BLUE WOLF

One night, Lobo, the wolf, went down to the home of Farmer Davis.

The farmer's wife had that day been using some blue dye. "I will leave it here in this tub," she said. "I may want it in the morning."

As Lobo jumped over the fence he fell into the tub.

"Dear me!" He said. "What is this? My fur is all wet with some queer stuff. I do not like it."

He tried to lick it off, but it tasted so bad that he soon stopped. He shook himself again and again, but still he could not get it out of his fur.

Next morning he went down to the pond and looked at himself

二十三
蓝色的狼

一天夜里,狼洛博去了农夫戴维斯的家。

那天,农夫的妻子一直在使用一些蓝色染料。"我应该把它留在桶里,"她说,"也许明天早上我还要用到它。"

当洛博跃过栅栏时,他掉进了桶里。

"哎呀!"他说,"这是什么呀?我的毛都被一些奇怪的东西弄湿了,我不喜欢它。"

他试图把它舔掉,但它的味道太差了,他很快就停下了。他一遍又一遍地摇晃着自己的身子,但他仍然无法从皮毛中抖掉这些东西。

第二天早上,他走到池塘边,看了看水中的自己。

"哎唷!"他说,"我变成了蓝色的。那些东西让我棕色

in the water.

"Why," he said, "I am blue. That stuff has made my brown fur turn blue. What shall I do? What will the other wolves say when they see me? I don't want them to see me. I think I will run away."

So he went to the other side of the mountain and stayed there three days.

Then he said, "I don't like it here. I want to go home. I know what I will do. I will play a trick on the other animals."

So he went back home, but he walked slowly and did not speak to anyone.

The other animals all came to look at him. They did not know that it was Lobo.

"What a queer animal!" Said Reynard. "Who can he be? I never saw a blue animal before."

"He looks very strange," said the goat. "Do you think he will eat us?"

"I am afraid of him," said the monkey. "I don't like the color of his fur."

After the animals had all looked at him and talked about him,

的皮毛变成了蓝色，我该怎么办呀？别的狼看到我后会怎么说我啊？我不想让他们看到我，我想我必须逃走。"

所以他只好去了山坡的另一边并在那里待了三天。

这时他说："我不喜欢待在这里，我要回家。我知道我该做什么，我要跟其他动物搞个恶作剧。"

就这样，他回到了家。不过，他走得很慢而且没有和任何人说话。

其他的动物都来看他，他们不知道那就是洛博。

"真是个古怪的动物啊！"列那说，"他究竟能是谁呢？我以前从没见过蓝色的动物。"

"他看起来很不寻常啊！"山羊说，"你们觉得他会吃掉我们吗？"

"我好害怕他！"猴子说，"我不喜欢他皮毛的颜色。"

当所有的动物都看过他并议论完之后，洛博坐下来并把他们叫到他的身边来。

"听我说！"他用一种陌生的声音说，"我是来做你们的国王的。难道你们看不出我和你们谁都不一样吗？我有蓝色的皮毛。没有其他的动物有这样的皮毛，这是国王的特权。列奥，那头狮子，他都没有这样的皮毛。我要在此占地称王。"

Lobo sat down and called them to him.

"Listen to me," he said in a strange voice. "I have come to be your king. Don't you see that I am different from any of you? I have blue fur. No other animal has such fur. It is only for kings. Leo, the lion, hasn't such fur. I will be king in this place."

"Good!" Cried some of the animals. "It will be fine to have a king with blue fur."

But some of the wolves talked together.

"I think he looks like us," said one wolf.

"Do as I say," said an old wolf. "Slip up behind him and give the howl of the pack. If he is a wolf he will answer. Then we shall know who he is."

So the wolves slipped up behind him. Then all together they gave a loud howl.

Before he thought Lobo answered.

"Ho, ho, Lobo!" Cried the wolves, "we know you."

"You are not a king!" Cried the other animals.

"Blue fur will not make a king of a wolf," said Reynard.

"太好了！"有些动物叫喊道，"有一个蓝色皮毛的国王应该是一件好事儿啊。"

不过还有几只狼一起议论起来。

"我觉得他看起来跟我们很像呢……"一只狼说。

"照我说的做！"一只老狼说，"悄悄走到他身后，然后发出狼群的长嚎。如果他是狼，他就会回答。那样的话，我们就会知道他是谁了。"

就这样，群狼悄悄溜到他身后，随后他们全体一起发出了一阵长嚎。

洛博不假思索就回答了。

"嗬，嗬，你是洛博！"群狼叫喊起来，"我们认出你来了。"

"你不是国王！"另一些动物喊叫起来。

"就算有蓝色的皮毛，也不可能变成狼群的国王。"列那说。

24
THE LION AND THE MOUSE

One day, Leo, the lion, lay down by his den.

"I am so tired," he said. "I am going to take a nap."

He was soon fast asleep.

A mouse lived near Leo's den. She was hurrying home to her little ones. She thought the lion's paw was a root and ran across it.

This woke the lion up. He was angry and roared loudly. The mouse was so frightened that she could not move.

Then Leo raised his big paw and put it down on the poor little mouse.

She squealed and squealed.

"Oh, please, Leo, let me go," she begged.

二十四
狮子和老鼠

有一天,狮子列奥躺在他的巢穴旁。

"我太累了,"他说,"我要小睡一会儿。"

他很快就睡着了。

一只老鼠住在列奥的巢穴附近,她正忙着回家去照看她的孩子。她以为狮子的爪子是树根,就跑着穿了过去。

这下把狮子给弄醒了。他生气地大声吼叫起来,老鼠吓得动弹不得。

这时,列奥抬起他的大爪子,把它放在了可怜的小老鼠身上。

她一遍又一遍地尖叫起来。

"哦,求求你了!列奥,让我走吧。"她恳求道。

"No, I will not let you go," said Leo. "You woke me up, and I am going to eat you."

"I did not mean to wake you up, Leo," said the mouse. "I thought your paw was a root. Please do not eat me."

"But I am hungry," said Leo. "I want something to eat."

"Oh, I am so small, Leo! It would take a hundred mice to take a dinner for you. Let me go and I will do something for you some day."

"不，我不会让你走的！"列奥说，"是你把我弄醒了，我要吃了你！"

"我不是故意把你弄醒的，列奥，"老鼠说，"我还以为你的爪子是个树根呢。请不要吃我啊！"

"可是我饿了，"列奥说，"我想要吃点儿东西。"

"哦，我太小了，列奥！弄来上百只老鼠也不够你吃一顿的。让我走吧，况且，说不定哪天，我也许能为你做点儿什么呢。"

"这真是一个天大的笑话！"列奥说，"你觉得像你这样一只小老鼠能为我做什么？"

"我不知道，列奥，"她说，"可是，请放我走吧。"

"好吧，这次我愿意放你走，"列奥说，"但不要在我睡着的时候再弄醒我了。"

老鼠逃回了家看她的孩子去了。

第二天，列奥外出打猎。他还没走出多远就被猎人们设置的罗网给捉住了。

他不断地吼叫起来。

老鼠正在她那个小房子的门口。

"我想知道，那会是什么声音呢？"她说，"一定是列奥

"That is a good joke," said Leo. "What do you think a little mouse like you could do for me?"

"I don't know, Leo," she said, "but please let me go."

"Well, I will let you go this time," said Leo. "But don't wake me up again when I am asleep."

The mouse ran away to her home and her little ones.

The next day Leo went out to hunt. He had not gone far when he was caught in the net of some hunters.

He roared and roared.

The mouse was at the door of her little home.

"I wonder what that noise is," she said. "It must be Leo. How he roars! Something must be the matter. I think I will go and see."

She ran toward the woods and soon found the lion.

"Why, Leo," she said, "what is the matter?"

"I am caught in this net," said Leo, "and I can't get out. Soon the hunters will come and kill me."

"Can't you break those ropes?" Asked the mouse.

"No, they are too strong," said Leo. "I am afraid I shall have to die."

吧。看他吼得多么厉害啊！一定是出了什么事，我想我应该过去看看。"

她跑向树林，很快就找到了狮子。

"啊唷，列奥，"她说，"这是怎么回事呀？"

"我被这张网捉住了！"列奥说，"我出不去了，很快猎人就会赶来杀死我的。"

"你不能撕碎那些绳索吗？"老鼠问道。

"不行啊，它们太结实了！"列奥说，"恐怕我是必死无疑了。"

"Let me help you," she said. "I think I can gnaw some of the ropes. Hold still, Leo. Don't roar so."

Then she used her sharp little teeth.

Soon one of the ropes was cut, then another and another.

"I think I can break the others," said Leo. "Now I am free. Thank you, dear little Mouse; you saved my life."

"You see I did help you, Leo," she said, "even though I am only a mouse."

"让我来帮帮你！"她说，"我想我可以啃断几根绳子。静下来别动，列奥，别这么使劲叫。"

这时，她锋利的小牙齿发挥了作用。

很快，其中一根绳子被咬断了，接着一根又一根。

"我想我能够扯碎其他绳子了。"列奥说，"现在我自由了。谢谢你，亲爱的小老鼠，你救了我的命啊！"

"你看，我确实帮了你吧，列奥，"她说，"尽管我只是一只老鼠。"

25

REYNARD AND THE HEN

One moonlight night Reynard started out hunting.

"I think I know how to get a good fat hen tonight," he said to himself.

He met Bruin on the road.

"Where are you going?" Asked the bear.

"I am going to the henhouse for a nice fat hen," said Reynard.

"You'd better be careful," said Bruin. "Farmer Davis has bought a new dog. He is a great big fellow and is not afraid of any animal. He nearly caught Lobo last week."

"I am not afraid," said Reynard. "I know a trick or two."

Soon he reached the henhouse.

二十五
狐狸和母鸡

一个月夜，列那外出打猎。

"我想我知道今晚如何能捉到一只又大又肥的母鸡。"他自言自语道。

在路上他遇到了布鲁因。

"你要去哪里啊？"熊问道。

"我正要去鸡舍抓只美味的肥鸡呢。"列那说。

"你最好小心点儿！"布鲁因说，"农夫戴维斯买了一条新狗。那是一个超乎寻常的大家伙，不惧怕任何动物。他上周差点儿逮住了洛博。"

"我不怕！"列那说，"我还是会几招儿的。"

很快，他就到了鸡舍。

High on a perch was a fine young hen.

"There is my supper," said Reynard, "but how can I get it? I shall have to try a trick."

Then he called softly, "Madam Hen, Madam Hen, wake up! Have you heard the news?"

"What news?" Asked the hen.

"Good news," said Reynard.

"What is it?" Asked the hen.

"King Leo has made a new law," said Reynard.

"I have not heard of it," said the hen.

"I have come to tell you about it," said Reynard. "King Leo says that no animal shall kill any other animal. He says that all animals and birds must be good friends."

"That is fine news," said the hen. "I am so glad to hear it."

"Come down here, Madam Hen, and I will tell you more about it," said Reynard.

"Listen!" said the hen. "I think I hear someone coming."

"Who is it?" Asked Reynard.

"I think it is the dog," said the hen.

栖木的高处有一只年轻漂亮的母鸡。

"我的晚餐有啦！"列那说，"可是我怎么才能抓到它呢？我必须要试上一招儿。"

于是，他轻柔地招呼道："母鸡女士，母鸡女士，醒一醒吧！你听到这个消息了吗？"

"什么消息呀？"母鸡问道。

"好消息啊。"列那说。

"什么好消息呀？"母鸡问道。

"国王列奥制定了一项新法律。"列那说。

"我还没听说过它呀。"母鸡说。

"我来就是要告诉你这个事儿的。"列那说，"列奥国王说了，任何动物都不得杀害其他动物；他说，所有的动物和鸟类都必须得成为好朋友呢。"

"这真是个好消息啊！"母鸡说，"我听到它真的太高兴了。"

"飞下来吧，母鸡女士，我会告诉你更多的事儿。"列那说。

"你听！"母鸡说，"我想我听到有人过来了。"

"谁来了？"列那问道。

"我想是那条狗吧。"母鸡说。

"我必须得走了。"列那说。

"I must go," said Reynard.

"Why do you hurry?" Asked the hen. "I was just coming down. Stay and talk the good news over with the dog."

"I haven't time to talk to him now," said the fox.

"Wait a minute," called the hen. "Here he comes. I am sure he will want to meet such a good friend."

But Reynard was running as fast as he could.

"I should like to stay," he called back, "but I am afraid the dog may not have heard of the new law."

"这么急着走干吗呀？"母鸡问道，"我正要飞下来呢。你还是留下来和那只狗详细讨论一下那个好消息吧。"

"我现在没时间跟他讨论。"狐狸说。

"再稍等一下吧，"母鸡叫道，"他来了！我可以肯定他乐意见到这么好的朋友。"

可是列那正以最快的速度逃跑呢。

"我倒是想留下来，"他回头喊道，"不过呢，恐怕那只狗可能还没有听说过那项新法律呢。"

26

HOW LOBO TOOK CARE OF THE SHEEP

Lobo, the wolf, saw a flock of sheep on the side of the mountain.

"What fine sheep those are!" He said to himself. "I hope Leo or Bruin will not find them. I want them for myself. I wonder how I can get them."

He watched them all day, but the shepherd was with them and Lobo did not dare go very near.

The next day he came again and watched them. The shepherd saw him and said, "there is the wolf that was here yesterday. If he comes nearer I shall kill him."

Just then Reynard came along.

"I will drive him away," said Lobo.

二十六
狼是如何照顾羊群的

狼洛博在山坡上看到了一群羊。

"那是些多么健壮的羊啊!"他自言自语道,"我可不希望列奥和布鲁因发现它们,我要独享它们;我想知道我怎样才能得到它们。"

他整天注视着羊群,但牧羊人一直和它们在一起,洛博不敢靠太近。

第二天,他又来监视它们。牧羊人看见了他,说:"昨天的那只狼来了,如果他再靠近一点儿,我一定杀了他。"

就在这时,列那走了过来。

"我必须把他赶走!"洛博说。

他冲向列那,迫使他回到树林里,然后他回来守候着羊。

He ran at Reynard and made him go back to the woods. Then he came back and watched the sheep.

"That must be a good wolf," said the shepherd. "He drove away the fox. I believe he wants to help me."

The next day Bruin came from the other side of the mountain.

"There is the bear that stole a lamb last week," said the shepherd.

Lobo ran at the bear. He bit him until Bruin was glad to run away.

"那一定是一只好心的狼!"牧羊人说,"他赶走了狐狸,我相信他是想要帮助我。"

第二天,布鲁因从山那边过来了。

"有一只熊上周偷走了一只羊羔儿。"牧羊人说。

洛博冲过去一阵撕咬,熊能逃开算它幸运。

"好能干的洛博!"牧羊人说,"你比一打狗都要强得多。"

每天洛博都来守护着羊,牧羊人每天都让他走近一点儿。

有一天,牧羊人说:"洛博,你真是一只好心的狼,你

"Good Lobo," said the shepherd, "you are better than a dozen dogs."

Everyday Lobo came and watched the sheep, and everyday the shepherd let him come a little nearer.

One day the shepherd said, "Lobo, you are such a good wolf; you can watch the sheep as well as I can. I must go to town this afternoon. You take care of the sheep. Don't let Bruin or Leo get any of them."

Then the shepherd went away and Lobo was left with the sheep.

"This is just the chance I have been waiting for," said Lobo.

He sprang among the sheep and killed a large number of them.

After he had eaten as many as he could he started for the woods.

"I think the shepherd will soon be home," Lobo said to himself. "He may be a little cross when he gets here. I don't think I care to see him."

When the shepherd returned he found that Lobo was gone and many of the sheep were killed.

"It serves me right," he said, "for trusting my sheep to a wolf."

可以像我一样照管好羊的。我今天下午必须要到城里去一下，由你来照顾这些羊吧，不要让布鲁因和列奥抓到任何一只羊。"

于是，牧羊人走了，留下洛博和羊在一起。

"这正是我一直等待的机会啊！"洛博说。

他跳到羊群中杀死了好多好多的羊。

在吃足了东西之后，他朝树林方向走去。

"我想牧羊人很快就要回家了。"洛博自言自语道，"等他来了，他或许会有点儿生气，可我才不管他呢。"

当牧羊人回来时，他发现洛博不见了，许多羊都被杀死了。

"我真是活该啊！"他说，"竟把我的羊托付给了狼……"

27
THE HARE AND THE TORTOISE

One day the brown hare met a tortoise. He had never seen one before.

"What a queer fellow you are!" Said the hare. "What short legs you have! Can you run?"

"I cannot run very fast," said the tortoise, "but I can beat some animals."

"How funny!" Said the hare. "Now, Mr. Tortoise, I should like to know what animal you could beat?"

"Well, Mr. Hare," said the tortoise, "I could beat you."

The hare laughed and laughed.

"That is the best joke I have ever heard," he said. "You must be

二十七
野兔和乌龟

一天，一只棕色的野兔遇到了一只乌龟，他以前从来没见过这家伙。

"你真是个古怪的家伙啊！"野兔说，"你的腿真短啊！你能跑吗？"

"我跑得不是很快，"乌龟说，"但我还是能战胜某些动物的。"

"这太好笑了！"野兔说，"此刻，乌龟先生，我倒是想知道你能击败什么动物呢？"

"这个嘛，野兔先生，"乌龟说，"我能战胜你！"

野兔止不住大笑起来。

"这是我听过的最好的笑话了！"他说，"你一定是疯了。"

crazy."

"No, I am not crazy," said the tortoise. "I know what I am talking about. Shall we race, Mr. Hare?"

"All right, I will race," said the hare, "but it is very funny."

"There is the fox over there in the road," said the tortoise. "Ask him to come and see that the race is fair."

"Oh, Reynard," called the hare, "come here. This silly tortoise wants to run a race with me. Isn't that a joke? We want you to tell us when to start and how far to run."

"All right," said the fox. "I like to see races. Do you see that big tree down there in the road? The one who gets there first wins the race. Now get back here on this line. Start when I count three. Now, ONE, TWO, THREE!"

When Reynard said "Three," away they both went.

The hare jumped along for a minute or two, then he looked around.

"I wonder where that tortoise is," he said to himself. "The idea of thinking that he could race with me! It is hot today. What is the use of my going so fast? I will lie down and take a little nap."

"不，我没疯！"乌龟说，"我知道我在说什么。我们比赛好吗，野兔先生？"

"好吧，我愿意比赛。"野兔说，"不过，这太滑稽了吧。"

"有一只狐狸在马路那边，"乌龟说，"叫他来见证一下我们是在公平竞赛。"

"哦，列那，"野兔叫道，"到这儿来。这只傻傻的乌龟想和我赛跑，这不是开玩笑吗？我们希望您告诉我们什么时候开始跑、跑多远。"

"好吧，"狐狸说，"我太喜欢看比赛了。你们看到马路那边的那棵大树了吗？第一个到达那里的人将赢得竞赛。现在，回到这条线上来吧，我一数到'三'你们就开始。好了，一——二——三！"

当列那数到"三"时，他们两个一起跑了出去。

野兔向前跳了一两分钟，然后他环顾了一下四周。

"我想知道那只乌龟跑到哪儿了。"他自言自语道，"他竟然会有和我赛跑这样的念头！今天这天气太热了，我跑这么快有什么用呢？我应该躺下小睡一会儿。"

可怜的乌龟被远远地抛在了后面。

"我知道我跑得不是很快，但我总会跑到树那里的。"他

The poor tortoise was left far behind.

"I know I cannot go very fast but I will get to the tree some time," he said to himself.

He moved slowly along the road. After a while he saw the hare.

"Why," he said, "here is the hare. I do believe he is asleep. How queer that he should go to sleep when he is running a race! If he will only sleep a little longer I can win."

After a while the hare woke up.

"Well," he said, "I had a good nap. I don't see that tortoise anywhere. I wonder if I slept too long."

He ran down the road as fast as he could.

When he reached the tree, Reynard and the tortoise were both there waiting for him.

"Slow and steady work wins the race," said Reynard.

自言自语道。

他沿着马路缓慢地前进。过了一会儿,他看到了那只野兔。

"哎唷!"他说,"这不是那只野兔嘛,我敢确信他是睡着了。这太奇怪了,他竟然在赛跑的时候睡着了!只要他多睡一会儿,我就会赢。"

过了一会儿,野兔醒了。

"好啦,"他说,"我这个小觉睡得好爽啊!我怎么在哪儿都看不到那只乌龟呢?我想知道我是不是睡得太久了……"

他以最快的速度沿路往下跑去。

当他到了树那边的时候,列那和乌龟两个都正在那儿等着他呢。

"虽然慢,但只要坚持不懈,就会赢得比赛!"列那说。

28

THE FROG AND THE MOUSE

A frog and a mouse once became good friends.

The frog lived most of the time in the water. He sometimes went to visit the mouse.

"I have such a nice home, Mrs. Mouse," said the frog one day. "I wish you would come and see where I live."

"But you live under the water," said the mouse. "I cannot go there for I cannot swim."

"I will teach you how to swim," said the frog.

"I am afraid I cannot learn," said the mouse.

"Oh, it is very easy," said the frog. "Just let me show you how. I'll tie your foot to mine with a piece of grass. Then I can drag you

二十八
青蛙和老鼠

有一只青蛙和一只老鼠曾经是好朋友。

青蛙大部分时间都生活在水里,他有时会去拜访老鼠。

"我有个非常好的家,老鼠太太,"有一天青蛙说,"我希望你能到我住的地方来看看。"

"可是你住在水下啊!"老鼠说,"我不能去那里呀,因为我不会游泳。"

"我愿意教你怎么游泳啊。"青蛙说。

"恐怕我学不会呀。"老鼠说。

"哦,这很容易的,"青蛙说,"看我教你怎么做吧。我会用一根草绳把你的脚绑在我的脚上,那样我就可以把你拽进水里了,直到你可以自己游泳。"

in the water until you can swim by yourself."

So the mouse went with the frog.

The frog laughed to himself. "What a good joke this will be on Mrs. Mouse!" He said.

Soon they came to the edge of the water. The frog gave a big leap. He went far under the water. Poor Mrs. Mouse went, too.

"Oh, Mr. Frog, I don't like this," she said. "Please take me to the shore."

But the frog only laughed.

"Come, let us swim some more," he said.

But the little mouse did not answer. She was dead.

The frog swam back and forth and jumped and played.

The dead mouse floated on the top of the water near him.

A fish hawk flew over the pond. She was looking for something to eat.

"Here is a dead mouse," she said. "I will take it home to my little ones."

The hawk picked up the mouse in her talons and flew away with it.

The frog had to go too, for his leg was still tied to the dead mouse.

"I wish I had not played that joke," he said.

于是老鼠就和青蛙一起去了。

青蛙暗自发笑。"这是和老鼠太太开了一个多么有趣的玩笑啊！"他说。

很快，他们来到了水边。青蛙奋力一跳，就在水下蹿出很远。可怜的老鼠太太也随着进入了水里。

"哦，青蛙先生，我不喜欢这样！"她说，"请带我上岸吧。"

但青蛙只是笑了笑。

"来吧，让我们再游一会儿。"他说。

但小老鼠没有回答，她死了。

青蛙在水里游来游去，又是跳跃又是玩耍。

死老鼠漂浮在他眼前的水面上。

一只鱼鹰在池塘上面飞过，她正在找吃的东西。

"这是一只死老鼠呀！"她说，"我会把它带回家给我的小孩子们吃。"

鱼鹰用她的双爪抓起老鼠，带着它飞走了。

青蛙也不得不跟着飞走了，因为他的一条腿仍然和那只死老鼠绑在一起。

"我真希望我没开过那个玩笑啊！"他说。

29

THE SICK LION

Leo, the lion, was sick. He stayed in his den all day.

He said, "oh, I am so sick! I cannot stand or walk. I can catch nothing to eat. I know I shall starve."

Just then a goat passed by.

"I wish I could catch that goat," said Leo to himself. "What a good dinner he would make!"

So he called as loud as he could, "oh, Goat, won't you come in to see me? I am sick and I want someone to talk to. Do come in for a little while."

The goat went into the lion's den. Leo caught him and ate him up.

二十九
生病的狮子

狮子列奥生病了,他整天待在兽窝里。

他说:"哦,我病得很重哟!我站不起来也走不了路,什么吃的都抓不到,我知道我就要饿死了。"

恰在这时,一只山羊路过。

"我希望我能抓住那只山羊,"列奥自言自语道,"他会给我提供一顿多么美味的晚餐啊!"

所以他尽可能大声地招呼道:"哦,山羊哟,难道你不愿意进来看看我吗?我生病了,我想要有个人和我说说话,你就进来一小会儿就行。"

山羊走进了狮子窝里,列奥抓住了他,把他吃掉了。

第二天,一只灰兔蹦蹦跳跳来到兽窝附近。

The next day a gray rabbit hopped along near the den.

"He is not very big," said Leo, "but I think I can catch him."

Then he called, "oh, little Rabbit, wait a minute. I haven't seen you for a long time. I am very sick. Won't you come in? I am all alone and I need someone to take care of me."

The rabbit hopped into the lion's den. Leo caught him and ate him up.

Next a big, white sheep came to the door and looked in.

"Oh, come in and help me," called Leo. "I am so sick that I think I am going to die. I am all alone. Please come in and sit by my side."

The big, white sheep went into the lion's den. Leo caught him and ate him up, too.

After a while Leo looked out of the door again. He saw Reynard, the fox, sitting at the other side of the road.

"How do you do, Reynard!" Called Leo. "Why don't you come over to see me? You know I am very sick. It does me so much good to see my kind friends. Do come in."

"No, thank you, Friend Leo," said Reynard. "I do not want

"他不是很大,"列奥说,"但我想我能抓住他。"

这时他招呼道:"哦,小兔子!等一下,我好久没见到你了。我病得很重,难道你不愿意进来吗?这儿只有我一个人,很孤单,我想有人来帮我一下。"

兔子跳进了狮子的窝里,列奥抓住了他,把他吃掉了。

接着,一只又大又白的绵羊来到门口往里看。

"哦,进来帮帮我吧!"列奥招呼道,"我病得很重,我想我就要死了。只有我一个人,很孤单。请进来,在我身边坐一会儿吧。"

大白羊走进了狮子的窝里,列奥抓住了他,把他也吃掉了。

to come to see you. I think it is better for me to stay out here. I see that the tracks of the goat and the rabbit and the big, white sheep all point toward your den. But I do not see their tracks pointing out again."

过了一会儿,列奥又向门外张望。他看到了狐狸列那,他正在马路的对面坐着。

"你好啊,列那!"列奥招呼道,"你为什么不能顺便过来看看我呢?你知道我病得很重,能见到我善良的朋友们,对我的病该是多么有好处啊!快请进来吧。"

"不,谢谢你,列奥朋友!"列那说,"我可不想进去看你,我认为我最好待在这外边儿。我看到山羊、兔子还有大白羊的脚印,都是走进你的窝里的,但没见到他们出去的脚印……"

30
THE WOLF IN SHEEP'S CLOTHING

As Lobo was going home one morning he met his cousin.

"Where are you going, Cousin?" He asked.

"I am going after some sheep, Lobo," said the other wolf. "Won't you go too? I know where there is a fine flock."

"I don't think I want to go," said Lobo. "I know where the flock is. The shepherd let me take care of the sheep once last summer. He does not like me very well now. I heard him say he would kill every wolf he could find. You'd better not go."

"I am not afraid," said the other wolf. "I know a new trick. I will fool the shepherd."

"How will you do it?" Asked Lobo.

三十
披着羊皮的狼

一天早上,洛博正往家走的时候,遇到了他的表弟。

"你要去哪里啊,表弟?"他问。

"我正要去抓羊,洛博。"另一只狼说,"你不想一起去吗?我知道一个地方,那里有一大群羊。"

"我想我还是不要去了吧。"洛博说,"我知道那群羊在哪里。去年夏天,那个牧羊人曾经让我照顾过那群羊。他现在恨死我了,我听他说,他要弄死他能发现的每一只狼,你最好别去了。"

"我不怕!"另一只狼说,"我掌握了一个新花招,我要骗一骗那个牧羊人。"

"你要怎么骗他?"洛博问道。

"I will tell you," said the wolf. "Last week I found the skin of a sheep. I am going to dress myself in it. Then the shepherd will think that I am a sheep."

"I am afraid he will kill you," said Lobo.

The wolf laughed and ran away.

That night he put on the sheep's skin. It covered him all over. He looked like a big, white sheep.

Next morning when the sheep were eating grass he slipped in among them. He pretended to eat grass too.

The shepherd did not notice him, and he stayed there all day.

Next morning when the shepherd was not looking he caught a lamb and ate it. The next day he ate a sheep. He did this for several days.

Then the shepherd counted the sheep.

"Some of my sheep and lambs are gone," he said. "Where can they be? I have not seen any wolves around."

The next morning he counted the sheep again.

"Two more sheep are gone," he said. "I do not understand it. Perhaps they are lost. I will go and look for them."

"我跟你说,"那头狼说,"上周我找到了一张羊皮。我要把它披在身上,到那时,牧羊人就会认为我是一只羊。"

"我担心他会杀了你。"洛博说。

那只狼笑了笑跑开了。

那天晚上,那只狼穿上了羊皮。羊皮将他整个都包裹起来,他看起来就像一只又大又白的羊。

第二天早上,当羊正在吃草时,狼溜进了它们中间,他也假装吃草。

牧羊人没有注意到他,所以狼一整天都待在那里。

下一个早上,趁牧羊人不留神的时候,他抓了一只羔羊并吃掉了它。过了一天,他又吃了一只绵羊。一连好几天他都是这样做的。

这时,牧羊人数了数羊。

"我的一些绵羊和羔羊怎么不见了呢?"他说,"它们究竟能去哪里呢?我在这周边没有看到有什么狼啊!"

第二天早上,他又数了一遍羊。

"又有两只羊不见了!"他说,"我真搞不懂,也许是它们迷路了,我应该去找找它们。"

牧羊人爬上了山,在一块岩石后面,他看到了两只羊。

The shepherd climbed up the mountain. Behind a rock he saw two sheep.

"There are my two sheep," he said. "But how queer! One of them is eating the other. I will find out about this."

Soon he saw that one of the animals was a wolf.

He struck the wolf with his club. Then he took a rope and hanged him on a tree.

"Now," said the shepherd, "I think you will not eat any more of my sheep."

Some men passed by.

"Why, Shepherd," they said, "what made you hang a sheep?"

"I did not hang a sheep," he said. "I hanged a wolf who was dressed in sheep's clothing."

"那正是我的两只羊呀!"他说,"可是,多么奇怪啊,它们当中的一只正在吃掉另一只!我必须要查清楚这是怎么回事儿。"

很快,他看清楚了,其中的一个正是一只狼。

他用棍棒猛击那只狼,接着他拿来一根绳子,把狼吊在了一棵树上。

"好了,"牧羊人说,"我想你再也吃不到我的羊了。"

有几个人从那儿路过。

"哎唷,牧羊人啊,"他们说,"你把羊吊起来干什么呀?"

"我没有把羊吊起来,"他说,"我吊起来的是一只披着羊皮的狼!"

31
HOW REYNARD LOST HIS TAIL

One day Reynard said to Lobo, "let us go hunting tonight. Farmer Davis has some nice, fat hens. They are easy to catch. We can get them as soon as it is dark."

"I don't think I will go with you, Reynard," said Lobo. "Farmer Davis has some new traps. Bruin told me so. He said that one of them nearly caught him. I am afraid of them. I don't want to go."

"I am not afraid of traps," said Reynard. "I never saw a trap that could catch me. An animal who gets caught in a trap is very stupid. Traps may catch bears and rabbits but they can't catch foxes. I am sorry you won't go with me."

As soon as it was dark, Reynard started for the henhouse.

三十一
狐狸的尾巴是怎么掉的

一天，列那对洛博说："让我们今晚去打猎吧，农夫戴维斯那里有几只肥美的母鸡。抓到它们轻而易举，等天一黑，我们就能得手。"

"我想我是不会和你一起去的，列那。"洛博说，"农夫戴维斯埋了一些新式的夹子，这是布鲁因告诉我的。他说其中有一个还差点儿捉住他。我害怕这些夹子，我可不想去了。"

"我才不怕夹子哪！"列那说，"我还从来没有见过可以捉住我的夹子哪。被夹子夹住的，都是些非常愚蠢的动物！夹子可以夹到熊和兔子们，但它们捉不到狐狸！你不能跟我一起去，我感到很遗憾。"

天一黑，列那就开始往鸡舍进发。

He said to himself, "Farmer Davis thinks he can catch me but he can't. I don't care for traps. I have never been caught in one yet."

Reynard was hungry and he ran as fast as he could.

Soon he came near the farmer's house.

"I will stop here a minute," said Reynard. "I think I smell something. Someone has been here. Oh, I see. Here is a trap. It must be the one Bruin was talking about. How very silly any animal must be to get caught in a trap like that!"

Reynard started away but suddenly the trap shut and snapped off his big, bushy tail.

Reynard howled and howled. Then he ran to the woods as fast as he could go.

"What shall I do?" He said

他自言自语道："农夫戴维斯自以为他能抓住我，但他做不到！我才不在乎什么夹子，我还从来没被哪个夹子夹住过呢。"

列那饿了，他以最快的速度跑了过去。

很快，他就来到了农夫家附近。

"我应该在这里停一会儿。"列那说，"我想，我好像闻到了什么，该是有人到这里来过。哦，我明白了，这里是一个夹子！这一定就是布鲁因说起的那个。会被这样的夹子夹住的动物该是多么愚蠢啊！"

列那刚要离开，但突然间夹子合上了，它"咔嚓"一声就夹断了狐狸那条毛乎乎的大尾巴。

列那一声接一声嚎叫起来。接着，他以最快的速度跑向了树林。

"我该怎么办呢？"他自言自语道，"其他动物都会嘲笑我的，因为我没有尾巴了。我不想让他们任何人看见我，我必须躲藏在灌木丛里。"

就这样，列那躲了很久。

这时，他想出了一个花招。他召唤其他所有的狐狸都来到他这里。当他们来了以后，他发表了演讲。但他站在那儿，后背一直靠着树。

to himself. "The other animals will all laugh at me because I have no tail. I don't want any of them to see me. I will hide in the bushes."

So Reynard hid for a long time.

Then he thought of a play. He sent for all the other foxes to come to him. When they came he made a speech, but he stood with his back against a tree.

He said, "My dear foxes, let us all cut off our tails. They are of no use to us. They are always in the way when we run through the bushes. I am sure we could all run faster without them. Let us cut them off at once."

"Why do you stand so close to the tree, Reynard?" Asked an old fox. "Turn around and let us see your tail."

But Reynard would not move. Then a big fox pushed him away.

"Look! Look!" Cried the old fox. "He has already lost his tail. All he wants is to help himself and not us."

他说:"我亲爱的狐狸们,让我们把尾巴都砍掉吧,它们对我们毫无用处。当我们穿过丛林时,它们总是碍事。我可以肯定地说,没有尾巴,我们大家可以跑得更快。让我们立刻切掉它们吧!"

"你为什么紧挨那棵树站着,列那?"一只老狐狸问道,"转过身来,让我们看看你的尾巴!"

但是列那不愿意动。这时,一只大狐狸把他推开了。

"看呀,看呀!"那只老狐狸喊道,"他的尾巴已经掉了。他想要的一切都是为了他自己而不是我们。"

32

THE CAT AND THE CHESTNUTS

Jocko and Pussy were one day taking a walk.

"Oh, see," said Jocko, "here is a fire which some hunters have left. Let us sit down and warm ourselves."

"I wish we had something to eat," said Pussy.

"Here are some chestnuts," said Jocko. "Let us roast them the way the men do."

"How is that?" Said Pussy.

"First you drop them on the coals, this way," said Jocko. "After they burst open I will show you how to get them out."

三十二
小猫和栗子

一天,黑猩猩乔科和小猫佩西正在散步。

"哦,看呀!"乔科说,"这里有一堆猎人留下的火,让我们坐下来取取暖吧。"

"我真希望我们能有点儿什么东西吃。"佩西说。

"这里有一些栗子。"乔科说,"让我们像人所做的那样把它们烤熟吧。"

"该怎么做呢?"佩西说。

"首先你要把它们丢到木炭上,就像这样。"乔科说,"等它们爆裂开以后,我会教你如何把它们取出来。"

"我从来没有吃过这东西!"佩西说,"它们很好吃吗?"

"哦,它们好吃极了!"乔科说,"这可比你吃过的任何

"I have never eaten any," said Pussy. "Are they very good?"

"Oh, they are fine," said Jocko. "You will like them better than anything you have ever tasted."

"I think they are done," said Pussy. "Now how do we get them?"

"That is easy, Pussy," said Jocko. "You take your paw and pull them out of the fire. Then I will break them open."

"But, Jocko," said Pussy, "the fire is so hot; I shall burn my paw."

"I am sure you can get the chestnuts if you try, Pussy," said Jocko. "Your paw is almost exactly like a man's hand."

Pussy was pleased at this. She reached for the chestnuts, but the coals burned her paw and she began to cry.

"Don't cry, Pussy," said Jocko. "Try again. You are so clever, I am sure you can get them."

Pussy tried again and again. At last she got three chestnuts out

东西都要好吃多了。"

"我想它们已经烤熟了。"佩西说,"现在,我们怎么把它们取出来呢?"

"这很容易,佩西。"乔科说,"用你的爪子把它们从火里掏出来,那样我就能把它们破开。"

"可是,乔科呀,"佩西说,"这火太热了吧,会烧到我的爪子啊。"

"我可以肯定,如果试一试,你是能取出栗子的,佩西。"乔科说,"你的爪子和人的手几乎完全一样。"

佩西听了很高兴。她伸爪子去取栗子,但木炭烧到了她

of the fire.

"I can't get any more, Jocko," she said. "My paw is dreadfully burned. Give me the three chestnuts. I want to taste them."

But Jocko had eaten the chestnuts when Pussy was not looking.

"A cat's paw," he said, "can pull chestnuts out of a fire better than anything I know of."

的爪子，她开始哭了起来。

"别哭了，佩西！"乔科说，"再试一次吧。你这么聪明，一定能把它们取出来的。"

佩西尝试了一次又一次，终于从火里取出了三个栗子。

"我不能再取了，乔科。"她说，"我的爪子被烧得糟透了。把那三个栗子给我吧，我想尝尝它们。"

但是，趁佩西没注意的时候，乔科已经把栗子给吃了。

"要说火中取栗，"乔科说，"猫爪子比我所知道的任何东西都管用。"

33

THE EAGLE AND THE TORTOISE

One day the tortoise saw an eagle. The eagle was high above him in the sky.

"How fine it must be to fly in the air like that!" Said the tortoise. "I am tired of crawling about on the ground. I want to learn to fly."

Soon the eagle came down near the tortoise.

"Oh, Eagle," said the tortoise, "won't you teach me how to fly?"

"Why, Tortoise," said the eagle, "you have no wings. How can you learn to fly?"

"I will try very hard to learn if you will only show me a little."

"You cannot fly," said the eagle. "Only birds can fly. You were made to crawl on the ground."

三十三
老鹰和乌龟

一天，乌龟看到了一只老鹰，那只老鹰高高地在他头顶上的天空中。

"能像那样在空中飞行该有多好啊！"乌龟说，"在地上爬来爬去的，烦死我了，我想要学会飞行。"

不久，老鹰就落到了乌龟旁边。

"哦，老鹰呀，"乌龟说，"您愿意不愿意教我飞行呢？"

"哎呀，乌龟，"老鹰说，"你没有翅膀，怎么能学会飞呢？"

"可如果您愿意给我一点点指教，我都会非常努力去学的。"

"你是不能飞行的，"老鹰说，"只有鸟儿才能飞，你天生

Then the eagle flew up in the sky.

The tortoise was unhappy because he could not fly, still.

The next day he went to the eagle again.

"Please teach me to fly," he said. "I want to go up in the sky as you do."

"You cannot fly," said the eagle. "Don't think about it any more."

The next day the tortoise came again.

"Eagle," he said, "I will pay you if you teach me to fly. I must learn."

Then the eagle was angry.

"When do you want your first lesson?" He said.

"Now," said the tortoise.

"All right," said the eagle. "First, I will take you in my claws and fly up in the sky."

When they were up high the eagle let go of the tortoise and said, "now fly."

Of course the tortoise could not fly. He fell down, down until he struck the rocks below.

就只能在地上爬。"

接着老鹰飞上了天空。

乌龟不高兴了，因为自己还是不能飞。

第二天，他又到老鹰那儿去了。

"请教会我飞吧，"他说，"我想要像你那样飞上天空。"

"你不能飞！"老鹰说，"不要再想这事儿了。"

又过了一天，乌龟又来了。

"老鹰呀，"他说，"如果你愿意教我飞，我会付钱给你的，我一定要学。"

这时，老鹰生气了。

"你想什么时候上第一节课？"他说。

"现在！"乌龟说。

"那好吧……"老鹰说，"首先，我会用爪子抓住你，然后就飞上天空。"

当他们高高在上时，老鹰松手放开了乌龟，说："现在——飞吧！"

当然了，乌龟不会飞。他往下掉，掉，直到摔在下面的石头上。

34

THE LION AND THE ECHO

Leo, the lion, came down the mountain one morning. He was looking for something to eat, but he could not find anything. This made him cross, and he growled loudly.

An echo growled back at him.

Leo was surprised.

"What was that?" He said.

He growled loudly again, and again his growl came back to him.

"I believe it is a man," he said. "I wish I could find him."

He crept softly through the woods. He could not find anyone.

He growled and then he roared.

Echo roared too.

三十四
狮子和回声

一天早上，狮子列奥从山上下来，他想找点儿吃的东西，却什么也没找到。这让他很恼怒，他大声吼叫起来。

吼声又传回到他这儿来。

列奥很惊讶。

"那是什么？"他说。

他又大声吼叫了一下，吼叫声再一次传回到他这儿来。

"我认为这是一个人！"他说，"我希望我能找到他。"

他轻手轻脚地爬过树林，却没有找到任何人。

他怒吼起来，接着他又咆哮几声。

回声也是一顿咆哮。

"那个听起来像是另一头狮子。"他自言自语道。

"That sounds like another lion," he said to himself.

Then he called as loud as he could, "whose voice is that which roars at mine?"

Echo answered, "mine."

This made Leo angry, and he called again, "who are you?"

Echo said, "who are you?"

"I am a great and strong lion," cried Leo.

"Lion," Echo answered.

Leo ran toward the voice and shouted, "come here and show yourself."

于是他尽可能大声地叫喊起来："是谁在出声对我咆哮？"

回声答道："咆哮——"

这让列奥生了气，接着他又叫了一声："你是谁？"

回声应道："你是谁？"

"我是一头又大又强壮的狮子！"列奥喊道。

"狮子——"回声答道。

列奥朝着声音方向跑去，大声喊道："到这儿来，让我看看你本人！"

"本人——"回声答道。

列奥更加生气了，他在树林里来回奔跑起来。他连吼带叫，回声也是又吼又叫。

"我懂了，那是另一头狮子。"列奥说，"他来到这里，想要成为我领地里的国王。但他不会成为国王的，我必须要找到他，然后我们会看到谁更强壮！"

列奥再次冲进树林。他咆哮的声音越大，咆哮的回声也越大。有时声音似乎来自树林的某个地方，但当列奥跑到那里时，回声却在另外一个地方。

那天早上，列那也在外打猎。他听到了列奥愤怒的咆哮，便过来看看是怎么回事儿。

"Elf," answered Echo.

Leo was still more angry. He ran back and forth through the woods. He growled and roared, and Echo growled and roared too.

"I know it is some other lion," said Leo. "He has come here and thinks he will be king in my place. But he shall not be king. I will find him, and then we shall see who is stronger."

Leo rushed through the woods again. The louder he roared the louder Echo roared. Sometimes the voice seemed to come from one part of the woods, but when Leo reached there Echo was in some other place.

Now Reynard was out hunting that morning, too. He heard the angry roars of Leo and came to see what was the matter.

"I think I will not go close to Leo just now," he said. "He is too cross."

So Reynard sat down behind a big rock. He saw Leo run through the woods. He heard him growl and roar, and he heard the answer of Echo.

At last Leo was so tired that he had to sit down and rest.

Then Reynard crept quietly through the bushes.

"我想,我这时候不该离列奥太近。"他说,"他正处在极度恼怒中。"

所以,列那在一块大石头后面坐了下来。他看到列奥在树林里穿梭奔跑,听到他又吼又叫,并且他听到了应答的回声。

终于,狮子累坏了,不得不坐下来休息。

这时,列那悄悄地从灌木丛中爬出来。

"列奥国王呀,"他说,"我可以告诉你一件事儿吗?"

"King Leo," he said, "may I tell you something?"

"What is it?" Asked Leo crossly.

"I do not think there is any other lion in the woods, Leo," said Reynard.

"There must be," said Leo. "Didn't you hear him roar? Just listen."

Leo gave a loud roar, and Echo sent the roar back.

"Yes, I hear it," said Reynard, "but, Leo, it is only your own voice that comes back to you in some queer way."

"That cannot be," said Leo.

"I am sure it is so," said Reynard. "Listen and you will hear my voice come back, too."

Then he gave two sharp little barks.

Two barks came back from Echo.

"That is strange," said Leo. "Do it again."

This time Reynard gave three short yelps. Echo sent back three yelps. Then Leo tried, and again his roars and growls came back.

"I don't understand it," said Leo. "But perhaps you are right, Reynard. How queer that a big lion who is King should be afraid of his own voice!"

"什么事？"列奥生气地问道。

"我觉得树林里根本没有其他狮子，列奥。"列那说。

"一定有！"列奥说，"你没听到他咆哮吗？你听听看。"

列奥发出一声咆哮，咆哮的回声传了回来。

"是的，我听到了。"列那说，"但是，列奥，那只是你自己的声音以某种奇怪的方式传回了你这里。"

"那不可能！"列奥说。

"真是这样的。"列那说，"听一下，你能听到我的声音也会传回来。"

然后他发出两声短促的尖叫。

两声尖叫的回声传了回来。

"这太奇怪了，"列奥说，"你再来一次。"

这一次列那发出了三声短促的尖叫，三声尖叫的回声传回来了。接着，列奥试了试，结果他的咆哮和吼叫声再一次传了回来。

"我弄不明白了……"列奥说，"但也许你是对的，列那。一头身为国王的大狮子，竟然会害怕他自己的声音，这是多么奇怪啊！"

附录

本书中出现的常用英语单词表
（共 666 个单词）

a	alone	anywhere	because	bite
about	along	are	become	blood
above	already	around	before	blow
advice	always	as	beg	blue
afraid	am	ask	begin	bone
after	among	asleep	behind	both
afternoon	and	at	believe	bother
afterward	angry	away	below	bottom
again	animal	back	bell	branch
against	another	be	best	bread
ahead	answer	bear	better	break
air	any	beast	big	breakfast
all	anything	beat	bird	bridge
almost	anyway	beautiful	bit	bright

bring	chew	cousin	different	eat
broad	city	cover	dining	edge
brother	claw	crawl	dinner	else
burn	clear	crazy	dish	enough
burst	clever	creep	divide	equal
bury	climb	cross	do	even
bush	close	crumb	door	ever
but	clothing	crust	down	every
buy	club	cry	dozen	everything
by	coal	curl	drag	exact
cake	cold	cut	dreadful	except
call	color	dance	dress	excuse
can	come	dare	drink	expect
care	cook	dark	drive	eye
careful	cool	day	drop	face
carry	corn	dead	dry	faint
catch	corner	deal	dye	fair
chance	count	dear	each	fall
chase	country	death	early	far
cheese	course	die	easy	farmer

farther	flesh	front	grow	hide
fast	float	full	growl	high
fasten	flock	fun	guard	hill
fat	fly	fur	had	him
father	follow	gauzy	hair	himself
feed	fond	get	hand	his
feel	foolish	give	hang	hit
fellow	food	glad	hard	ho
fence	fool	glare	hardly	hold
few	foot	gnat	has	hole
field	for	gnaw	have	home
fight	fore	go	he	honey
find	forest	good	head	hope
fine	forth	grain	hear	horse
finish	free	grass	heavy	hot
fire	fresh	gray	help	house
first	friend	great	hen	how
fish	fright	greedy	her	hundred
fix	frighten	green	here	hungry
flat	from	ground	herd	hunt

hurry	kind	lesson	man	more
hurt	king	let	manger	morning
I	kitchen	lick	many	most
if	knife	lie	mark	mother
idea	know	life	master	mountain
in	lake	light	matter	mouth
indeed	large	like	may	move
instead	last	line	me	Mr.
into	late	lip	meal	Mrs.
is	later	listen	mean	much
it	laugh	little	meat	muddy
jar	law	live	meet	music
jaw	lay	lone	meeting	must
joke	lead	long	might	my
juice	leaf	look	mind	myself
jump	leap	lose	mine	name
just	learn	loud	minute	nap
keep	leave	love	mistake	narrow
kid	left	madam	money	near
kill	leg	make	moon	nearly

neck	oh	perhaps	put	roar
need	old	pet	quarrel	roast
never	on	pick	queer	rock
new	once	pie	queen	room
news	one	piece	quick	root
next	only	pile	quiet	rope
nibble	open	pity	quite	rough
nice	or	place	race	rub
night	other	plan	raise	run
no	out	play	rather	rush
noise	over	please	reach	same
noon	own	pleased	ready	save
nose	pack	plenty	refuse	say
not	pantry	point	reply	see
nothing	part	polite	rest	seem
notice	pass	pond	return	seize
now	paw	poor	right	selfish
number	pay	pretend	ring	send
of	peck	pull	river	serve
off	perch	push	road	settle

several	silk	sorry	still	taste
shade	silly	sound	strange	teach
shadow	since	soup	stream	tear
shake	sister	sour	strike	tell
shall	sit	speak	strong	terrible
share	skin	speech	stuff	than
sharp	sky	spin	stupid	thank
she	sleep	spring	suddenly	that
shelf	slip	squeal	summer	the
shine	slow	stand	supper	their
shore	smell	start	sure	them
should	snap	starve	surprise	then
shoulder	snow	stay	sweet	there
shout	so	steal	swell	they
show	soft	steady	swim	thin
shut	some	step	sword	thing
side	something	stick	take	think
sick	sometimes	still	tail	third
sight	song	sting	talk	thirsty
sing	soon	stop	tall	this

those	track	use	wheat	wood
thousand	tree	very	when	wool
thread	tremble	visit	where	word
three	trick	voice	which	work
throat	trouble	wait	while	worn
through	trust	wake	who	worth
tie	try	walk	whose	would
time	tub	want	why	wound
tip	tune	warm	wide	year
tired	turkey	was	wife	yes
to	turn	watch	wing	yesterday
today	two	water	will	yet
together	under	way	win	you
tongue	understand	weak	winter	young
tonight	unhappy	wear	wise	your
too	unless	week	wish	yourself
tooth	until	web	with	
top	up	well	without	
toward	upon	wet	wonder	
town	us	what	wonderful	